P9-CES-057

Verging on the Pertinent

STORIES BY CAROL EMSHWILLER

COFFEE HOUSE PRESS :: MINNEAPOLIS :: 1989

Some of these stories first appeared in the following magazines: *New Directions Annual* 42, *Croton Review, Portland Review, Confrontation, 13th Moon, Pulpsmith, TriQuarterly, PsyCritic, Voice International Literary Supplement,* and *Ascent*. "Escape is No Accident" appeared in *The American Tricentennial,* edited by Edward Bryant.

Cover illustration by Janice Perry.
Back cover photo by Jamie Spracher.
The glyphic illustrations by Carol Emshwiller for "There Is No God But Bog" and "Expecting Sunshine and Getting It" were redrawn by Kent Aldrich.

Written with the help of a National Endowment for the Arts Grant, and a New York State Foundation for the Arts grant.

The publisher thanks the following organizations whose support helped make this book possible: The National Endowment for the Arts, a federal agency; the Dayton Hudson Foundation; Cowles Media/Star Tribune; and United Arts.

Coffee House Press books are distributed to trade by Consortium Book Sales and Distribution, 287 East 6th Street Street, Saint Paul, Minnesota 55101. Our books are also available through all major library distributors and jobbers, and through most small press distributors, including Bookpeople, Bookslinger, Inland, Pacific Pipeline, and Small Press Distribution. For personal orders, catalogs or other information, write to:
Coffee House Press
27 North Fourth Street, Suite 400, Minneapolis, Mn 55401.

Library of Congress Cataloging in Publication Data
Emshwiller, Carol.
Verging on the Pertinent : stories / by Carol Emshwiller.
p. cm
ISBN 0-918273-57-9 : $9.95
I. Title.
PS3555.M54V47 1989
813'.54--DC20

Contents

Yukon

He's a dragon. He's a wolf. He's caribou. She tries to please him. She tries to keep out of his way and, at the same time, tries to get him to notice her by doing little things for him when he's gone or asleep. She needs him for warmth so they can cuddle up and he can warm her. She's afraid to leave because that's all the warmth she has. But she's afraid to stay. Is it possible to rush away when you live this far north? These high valleys never get warm. Mountain water coming down from glaciers is bright turquoise.

He's always looking at the sky or the ground or the horizon, not at her. But bits of red wool is all she has to look good in and then she never was a popular girl. If had big fur boots and hat, then maybe make a move. Make a run for it.

As valley to mountain top . . . might as well be ship-to-shore, sending signals. How live that way. How love?

He's a rattlesnake, but no immediate threat (that she can tell). Comes home when he feels like it, bringing dead things to eat. Holds conventional views. Passes judgments on. Everything that needs to be said, he says, already said, and she thinks he's probably right, or almost. Make him chopped liver. Make him hasenpfeffer. Make him big mugs of glogg, but might not be home till three AM anyway. Wait up. And always those Englemann spruce. A couple of hundred years old—even more—but still skinny. Nothing to them. She loves them, though what else is there to love? It's the only tree around.

He's a giant. He's a dwarf. She has to help him climb up onto his throne. For the love of the spruce trees, she nuzzles into his furry chest, thinking that to love him you have to love horses, spiders, and raw oysters, thinking how now she's going to have a baby. Should she tell him? She's already fairly big-with-child, but he hasn't noticed. She decides not to tell him. She decides, boy or girl, she will name it Englemann as though they were Mr. and Mrs. Spruce.

Their mansion is unfinished still. Only the vestibule built (but it's a big one, even as mansion vestibules go) and one tower (small) from which to view the mountains above the tops of trees. Both vestibule and tower are made out of the local rocks, so on the walls are the faint etchings of trilobites and prints of the leaves of ancient, ginkgo-like trees. In the fireplace they stand out clear, outline by the smoke. Once upon a time it was warm here, and covered with water. The land has shifted, quake by quake, away from some southern latitude and it's still going. North by northwest. Also rising straight up. On land such as this, it's easy to go astray.

And now she's going just a little big crazy. She wants and wants. Stands at window as if caged. Plastic that's in front of the glass to keep the heat in, makes things fuzzy. Snow outside begins to look soft and warm. Just right. So she leaves. She's not so crazy she doesn't take cheese sandwiches, peanuts, raisins, carrots . . . . Also takes his big fur boots and hat and now she's out in those nice adolescent-looking spruce trees that are older . . . much, much older than they look. She hugs some (though not much to hug). Touches them as she goes by. Wants to soak up the stolid way they are and also wants them to know how she feels: that even though they're stunted because of their hardships, she loves them all the more for it. She stops to drink glacier milk along the way. She's following, at first, browse trails that go no special place. It's cold. She just goes on. Easy to go astray. Thinks: years of going astray . . . was always astray, so if now astray, it's no different from before.

Meanwhile he's home—just woke up and sitting by the fire she'd laid before she left, asking himself ultimate questions, or, rather, penultimate questions as, What about the influence of theory on action? What about negative ends versus positive means and vice versa? He doesn't notice she's gone, slipping around out there in his too-big-for-her boots. She had not meant to be going in a northerly direction. She had not meant to be climbing on up higher into the cold. She thought for a while she'd maybe creep back after he'd gone to sleep with no supper, but she's too far now for that. (He'll miss his boots before he'll miss her.) She was thinking: South and warm and down, down, into the lower valleys, but she's been going up because it's the hardest and she's always done whatever was the hardest. The spruce get older and smaller the higher she goes until there's—all at once—no more of them. Meanwhile he keeps putting on another log until the whole vestibule dances with the fire and he pulls off sweater after sweater, watches his giant shadow writhe along the walls, falls asleep in his chair.

If there had been flowers blooming up there on the mountains, she would have known the names of every single one. If birds had called out, she'd have known which birds and would have whistled back.

Since she'd started in the morning after a sleepless night (though all her nights have been sleepless for a long time. She can hardly remember the times when she used to sleep well). . . . Since she'd started early she gets almost all the way to the top before it's too dark to go on. She finds a kind of cairn built by summer climbers. There's a slit at the bottom big enough to slither into. She does. Sleeps, not well, but better than she's slept in a long time, dreaming: Loves me? Loves me not? And: Who (or what!) is number one in his heart? It's his boots, and his hat keeps her warm enough (or almost warm enough) all night, so in the morning she's (as usual) full of grateful love for him and wondering: Why hasn't he followed no matter how hard? Why hasn't he come for her by now with something nice and warm to drink? He's never done anything remotely like that, but still she wonders why he's not already there, maybe having climbed all night just for her.

She squirms out and, first thing, she sees she's almost to the top so goes on up. What she thought was five minutes' worth of climbing turns out to take a half an hour. At top she sits on fossils and looks out – little shivers of pleasure or of cold – eating raisins and soaking up comfort and courage from the view, this side, too: Englemann, Englemann, everywhere Englemann below her, first in the sheltered hollows and then, lower down, nothing but. Thinks: Nothing like them, and nothing like being up this high, and nothing like what it took to get this far, nothing like the cold, clear air. She even forgets she's pregnant.

Now, down in the big stone vestibule, he is shouting, "Bacon, bacon!" Searches what few crooks and crannies there are to search, groans and spits, hisses into the corner under the king-sized bed, makes his own black coffee, spends the morning writing out new rules while she walks the col, too exhilarated to feel fear of heights. One last bit of glacier still sits in the steep pocket below her. She can tell by the old blue ice showing where the pure white snow's been blown off. She follows the ridge above and then past, and then starts down, but she's being too courageous . . . too sure of herself now, falls, slides the whole bare slope till stopped . . . saved by one thin old Englemann, her knee twisted back behind. Hurts. Probably nothing broken though she's not sure. Waits, lying there clutching tree because of pain. She's looking straight up through the narrow, scraggly circle of branches to the sky that's clouding over, thinking: Tree, tree, *this* tree and sky. Ties her scarf tight around her leg. That helps. It's getting windier. Big black clouds off over next mountain. She must get lower and to some sheltered spot. Can't stop now. Gets up. Goes from tree to tree to tree (she's *depending* on them) steeply down. Thinks: If not for Englemann spruce to hang on to! . . . .

By late afternoon finds bear's cave still warm from that big body. She knows it's a bear's cave. She can smell it. She can see the footprints in the snow, people-like prints but wider, leading out. She needs the shelter now and the warmth of it. Can't go on. And she's more cold than scared. Also it's beginning to snow. She creeps in. Wedges herself among the tree roots along the left-hand side away from the more open part of the cave. She knows the bear will come back, but she thinks she already knows how to keep away from something big (or small) and dangerous. She falls asleep, a dreamless sleep, not so full of unanswered questions about love or the lack of it.

The bear comes back at three AM. She hears him sniffing around outside and giving little warning growls. Also he's got the hiccups. Nothing here she hasn't heard already, and many times. She's only half awake. Before she realizes it, she's told him she loves him. She's talking soft and low. He grunts, then hunkers on in, rolls to far side, back turned. (She thinks: As usual.) He lets her be. Snores. Storm goes on outside. Later (as usual) she moves close, snug against his back.

They sleep two days and nights, or so she guesses. When she wakes up later, as he's leaving, she finds he's eaten all her cheese sandwiches, carrots, peanuts and raisins, and she thinks: As usual.

She hurries to the entrance of the cave and calls out to him before he goes. Her knee hurts and maybe she's a little feverish. She speaks without thinking. That's not her usual way, but he seems a little bit safer than her own male, even though he's the biggest and most masculine thing she's ever been this close to (dangerous, too). No doubt about it. She does like his looks, though: his hump, his shoulders, his yellow-brown fur. . . . Now he hangs his head low, almost to the snow, and looks back at her suspiciously, and it isn't as if she hasn't seen that same look a thousand times before. But what is there to lose? She talks to him of things she'd never dared to talk about before. "How can love last," she says, "if this goes on? How can love even begin? How can it go on and on, and we all," she says, "want undying love. Even you, though you may not think so. It's normal. And, by the way," she says, "food is love, you know. Love is food. It's how we live. It's what we live by, and you've eaten it all up."

Needless to say she'd never said any such thing to her own overbearing, legal, lord and master, though she'd wanted to for a long time.

The bear watches her as she speaks, as though too polite to interrupt or move even. His little beady black eyes take everything in, that's clear. There's a dull, sleepy, intelligent look about him. He waits patiently until she's finished, then humps off in powdery snow.

She sucks ice from the cave entrance. Finds a piece of root to make a splint for her knee. After that makes a broom from root ends and tidies up, all the while chewing root hairs from the cave ceiling. When everything is spic-and-span she sleeps again. At three AM or thereabouts he comes back with a small black bass for her. It seems as if he's taken what she said to heart. She lets him have half though she knows he's already eaten (not only all her food, but lots more, too). He licks up the fish scales she leaves. He eats the head (she gets the cheeks and also swallows down the eyes, though that's not easy to do). While they eat she talks and talks like she never talked before. She tells him all she knows about bears and that she hopes to learn lots more. Later she rubs the back of his neck and behind his ears. Top of his head. She likes the feel of him, and he's so warm. It's like the fireplace is lit when he comes in. She sings and he hums back a tune of his own she learns by heart. (She loves the sound of his voice.) They sleep again, she can't tell how long. Next time he leaves, they kiss, and not just cheeks. When he comes back, he brings another fish. And it goes on like this except they're kissing more and sleeping longer and longer periods, breathing slowly into each other's faces and not even getting up to pee, he, not turning his back to her except now and then and, when he does, giving her a bear hug first. It's a whole other rhythm she'd never known about before. And not bad, she thinks, to let the storms go on by themselves and forget about everything and just be warm and cuddled and cuddling all the time. It's what she's always wanted: arms around her that hardly ever let go. It's what she didn't get when she was little.

They don't even feel the earthquake, though it shakes a little dirt and pebbles down on them. She dreams it, though, and in the dream the quake is her husband's big feet shaking the mountain as he comes to get her to tear her away from her embrace. Before that she'd sometimes dreamt that the storms are him, too, tearing at the cave to pull her out. When those dreams come, she hugs tighter to her bear and he embraces her yet more snugly. Then she knows she's safe and thinks she finally has all one needs of real love and that it will last forever though maybe that's too much to hope for.

Meanwhile, back at the vestibule, the earthquake has caused quite a bit of damage. Some walls have crumbled and part of the roof come down. The fireplace is still OK though. He can squat in front of it mooing for his woman, and he still has most of his tower from which to growl out at the moon or stars or sun. Now he'll have to clean up the debris by himself as well as cook, cut his own firewood, skin his own marmots. If she knew this she could feel some sweet revenge, or maybe, I-told-you-so, except she never had.

One starry winter night when her knee is better, though not completely, she limps out with her bear and it's so nice the bear stands up and does a little soft-shoe while she throws snowballs at the sky. She limps, but she can shuffle and wobble from tree to tree, kissing them and him. They're singing all the songs they know, but by now she's forgotten most of the words. Knows only rhyme and alliteration though she remembers the oxymorons, especially since "the brightness of midnight" is all around them right now. It's sharply cold, but even so they both know spring is in the air. After this night, they begin to sleep less and then she has the baby. He's so small and thin she hardly knows she's birthed him except she hears the peeping. The bear helps by licking it clean and then eats the placenta. By then it's not a question of naming it. She can't even remember what names are for.

It gets warmer and the bear's gone more and more and brings back less and less. The baby might as well be a little bird. Besides her own milk, she feeds it worms and grubs. She tweets at it and it tweets back. When the bear stays out six days in a row, she suspects she's made the same old mistake . . . same kind of destructive relationship she's always had before. He'll go for good. He'll forget about her. Or if he comes back, turn savage on her. Maybe push her out along with her robin, sparrow, little tufted titmouse.

Then, when he doesn't come back at all anymore, thinks: Yes, yes, she knew it would happen and now she'll have to go, too. Be out on her own. Find the next meal herself. It's a bright spring day, wild flowers coming out, but she no sooner starts down, baby perched on her shoulder, pecking at her ear, than it flies away and she has no name to call it back by. She tries to caw him down. She whistles all the bird calls she knows, but none work. He circles for a few minutes while she finds the words to tell him he can't fly, or anyway, not yet. It only wobbles him a little. He utters one harsh quack she'd never heard him make before, then soars away, out over the valley. She thinks she hears soft coos and cuckoos even after he disappears into the trees below.

Well, she'll just go down by herself. And south. But this other valley, not towards home. This time maybe not take the hard way, though she's wondering, as usual, Where is the creature with which she can live happily ever after?

Then she sees a figure climbing up. First it's just a greenish-brown slowly moving spot, but then it becomes green *and* brown . . . tweeds and corduroys. Thin, small, wiry. Has a greenish-gray beard. Alpine hat with little red feathers in it. Black-button bearish eyes. She sees them as he comes closer. Though she's never seen him before, she knows who it is. Knickers, hiking boots—the old-fashioned kind. "Englemann," she says, "Englemann, Englemann." It's one of the few words she's not forgotten . . . never would forget though she is, by then, almost free of words. She will have to start over now from the beginning with wah, bah, and boo.

He comes up the last switchback. They look at each other and smile. He has a little tuft of fragrant mountain misery in his buttonhole. He takes it out, sniffs it once, then gives it to her.

"Oh, Englemann," she says and, "wah" and "bah" and "boo."

Clerestory

> "It therefore follows that it was not art that was to blame on the day of the Lisbon earthquake . . ." (and as to art) "the people were not in the mood for it."
>
> —Dostoevsky

THAT THE STATUE should have been found at what might be called the very gates of the city seems to me appropriate, though this is not Troy, and our city has, being a modern city, no gates. It was found on a side street on Long Island. Uniondale, actually. No one had noticed it until my group did. We have members on the lookout in every borough and suburb. Almost nothing with the possibility of art escapes us.

But I want to make it clear that my group never considered the statue to be art as such. We are not confused by patinated surfaces. Though we called it cubistic, this was but a reference to its overall squareness and not that it might be a part of that movement. We knew it was not art qua art; but that it might be some sly form of it, awaiting but a pointing finger (LOOK!), was not completely out of the question. Strangely, though, I do not remember that considerations of its worth ever entered our minds. I don't believe we discussed its qualities or lack thereof even once. The statue surprised us and scared us and made us laugh — all qualities of art, that's true. But though it caused, indeed, a gasp of sorts, it was never a question that it was the gasp of art.

At first we had doubts that this was the statue of a woman, or even that it was a statue at all. The boxes that formed her armature were visible as a sort of cubistic underpinning and left some doubt, especially when viewed from certain angles, as to whether our find was little more than a row of squatters shacks; but standing back and squinting, some of us could see that the silhouette was, and quite clearly, hips, waist, then the elbow of the upraised arm which seemed to curl behind her head. When this had been affirmed by a majority of the members of my group, we rented a flatbed truck and towed the statue to the center of the city. There was some debate about taking it to Central Park (which might be considered the real center of the city), but it was decided in the end to take it to Washington Square because most of our group lives in that neighborhood.

We did not damage many trees along the route, though some groups say we did, namely the Trees as Treasures Association and the Citizens for the Embellishment of City Streets.

Even though she is neither art nor beautiful, when we finally raised her to her temporary plinth, we all cheered. Now that she is set up here, we believe she is as entitled to preservation as any other landmark.

People walk past her just as we almost did ourselves, as though she were nothing but a cluster of mismatched huts.

We set up a twenty-four-hour guard, one of us at a time, and so it was that I was the one watching over the statue early one morning when a door opened—opened in the left side and Ursula came out. I knew her only a little. She was the waitress at the corner diner. (As soon as I saw her come out, I remembered hearing her speak once or twice of going out to Uniondale.) She carried a laundry basket and strung a line from knee to knee (the statue's). Then, standing on its anklebone, she hung up sheets and underwear. I wanted her to be arrested on the spot, but no cops in view. I knew that some groups might say that laundry could be art—that it might need but that pointing finger, that "LOOK!"—but this is not my view. At least it wasn't then.

"Are you alone?" I asked, but that wasn't what I meant to say. "Are you part of this thing?" (What did I mean by that?) "Is it yours? You ought to be arrested."

I had taken a good look at her before in the diner. Though quite ordinary, she was my type. (I was glad I was wearing my suit, my brown Homburg. I knew I looked as though I had some authority over matters of art and the preservation thereof.)

If she had said, "I live with eleven swans or seven brothers," at that moment I would not have been surprised, but she just smiled and went on hanging things up. Smiled to herself, that is, not to me. And she was humming. It was one of those tunes that always makes me angry, even (or especially) when I find I am humming them myself: "Susie, Little Susie."

"It's wrong," I said. "You can't hang underwear here. You have to find another place. This is art."

I said it, though I knew it wasn't. I said it just to get my way. I said it also because I wanted — at least for that moment — I wanted it to be true, though I knew it couldn't be. And I thought she wouldn't know any better, being nothing but, or so I thought, a diner waitress.

"Have you asked permission," I said, "to hang things on art?"

I knew that such permission would not be granted if the statue were indeed of any merit whatsoever. And I knew that any object of importance should especially not be hung with intimate apparel and especially not when such apparel, though lacy, wasn't even new. Every bit of it was stretched and torn, pieces of lace dangling here and there; blacks, faded; whites, grayed; and, though washed, nothing seemed that clean.

"Permission!" I said, "Permission!" But she didn't answer.

"The statue is closed," I said, "until eleven-thirty."

Of course I was making all this up.

It was then she said what seemed to me to be "hippogriff," or "hippocampus" or perhaps only "hypocritical." And then she said, "Transferring hippopotami" (or whatever that word was) "to the same plane as landscapes." "From the start," she said, "not necessarily objects easily recognizable," and, "an hypothesis," she said, "so rich in unexpected effects."

I thought at once that she had read some of the same books I had, and I knew that now was the time I should say that the statue wasn't art — on the contrary, in fact — but I didn't say it. I let her go on thinking that I thought it was. All I answered was, "I know, I know," as though I did know.

When she turned and went back, she held the door open for me, that I should go on in first, but I didn't. I didn't want to even though she was my type.

But now, having said that it was art, I was seized with the desire to make it so . . . to make it shine with audacity and to raise it to its own idiosyncratic statement. I wanted to purify it, not of its ambiguities, but of its somewhat cross-eyed gaze. I wanted to equalize the breasts, build up the nose so that it would match the strength of the overhanging brow. And I wanted to make a sacrifice of hours and hours of labor and thought for the sake of what the statue might become. I hoped that those who saw me at work on this project and who had, perhaps, overheard me saying that the statue was art, would be astonished at the reality of my words and astonished that I, of all of us, had seen the statue as what it might become, and that I, of all of us, could work with such delicacy and persistence as would, of course, be required.

At this time I was a respected member of my group, known as finder, preserver, and measurer, but not as someone capable of the gestures that I had in mind. All my concerns had been for the loss of worthwhile objects, not to mention the loss of objects that might actually be art or that might have possibilities as art. Now, however, I hoped to be enmeshed in the very act of transforming the one into the other . . . one kind of worth or woman or statue of a woman into another kind. Also Ursula was, indeed, my type.

If I had stopped and thought about what work would give me the most pleasure, then it would have been this particular work and this particular kind of pleasure which I envisioned as the pleasure both of the structured and the free in a harmonious juxtaposition. I hoped to struggle with opposites and yet *not* resign them to each other. I thought I might title the work something like "The Persistence of Pleasure or, perhaps more realistically, "The Pleasures of Persistence."

The landmarks division had stipulated that the statue must be painted with one of the six landmark colors permissible. They had ordered that the "windows" — as they were referred to — of the blue, blue eyes be repaired and opened to the light, and that the pediment that is the brow be reinforced, the pilaster of the arm repaired, the tower of the upraised elbow made safe for at least four people.

Some fears are logical. I did not tell myself that I should not have them. It is normal to fear heights when one has never worked on scaffolding or ladders. It is normal to fear women.

I went out with Ursula the next weekend anyway. I suppose we made a strange couple — I in my suit and hat and she looking like some homeless waif. Considering that she lives in a statue, I suppose that's true, she is. She said she was thirty-six and never married. I didn't tell her I was forty because I worried that she might say I look even older.

As part of my project I asked her if she would let me change her hair-do and if she would wear clothes that I picked out for her. (When I saw her for the first time in a dress I'd chosen, I thought, yes, yes, this is work for the "common good.")

Soon after that I asked her if she'd pose nude, but she asked, "Why?" I tried to use logic: "For the sake of the common good. For a higher purpose than you or I can name," but there was no end to her whys. "Art makes anything permissible," I said. "It stops at nothing."

"Why?" she said.

"Why not!" I shouted.

I was on the scaffolding at that time, almost at the level of the shoulder. I had polished the wood of the entablature to a copperish luster and I had actually stood on the sills of the eyes while doing so. "I'll tell the truth," I said. "I'm scared. I'm scared of the risk and I don't know where all this will lead, but we both might be famous."

She knew enough about art not to argue with me about that, and I'm sure before I said it she had known I was afraid. Sometimes she had goaded me on up to the topmost scaffolding while she watched from the ground, her eyes fearless. But for all my resentment of her goading, I knew that art is never comfortable.

I had saved the most fearsome task for last. The head was, after all, second only to the elbow in height. Clearly brachycephalic. The suggestion of a headband crossed it ear to ear. I had already dealt with that by adding egg and dart. At one time we had been taught that decoration was beneath contempt. Eclecticism, the same. But I was not any longer convinced of the form-follows-function of the Doric, and I did not want to ignore the Impressionistic, nor even Dada and Pop. I thought, What if I did the hair in an exuberant and eclectic version of Corinthian? And I set about, then, in rock-climbing shoes and rope, rappeling myself about the head. During the course of this, I overcame, to a large degree, my acrophobia.

As it turned out, the city did not delight in this courageous hair, nor in any part of the statue. On the contrary. It took my gestures as mistakes and ignorance. Everyone wondered why I had, as it seemed to them, forgotten about the Ionic that topped each breast, and as it seemed to them, inadvertently switched to another mode. (Their very words.) I had not delighted or surprised or frightened anyone—except perhaps myself.

Also they said, "The pilaster is a lie." I knew that. But in this case the pilaster was not structurally dishonest at all, but a true arm and a true support. It was the breasts that were false. They supported nothing. They spoke (if one can say they speak at all) of the delights of pure form. They were "only" themselves.

I thought, then, of all the things I might have named my work that would have alerted the city to its meaning: "Assemblage," for instance, to show I knew very well what it was composed of; or "Uncomfortable Incongruity," or—and even more apt—"Object Not Easily Recognizable," for many of the people had not even known that it was the statue of a woman, just as we had not been sure of that ourselves when we first found it. Then, in a fit of Dada (though not entirely inappropriate) I wished I had called it "Hippopotamus."

Since I had not complied with any of the recommendations of the Landmarks Commission, they said they would not be responsible for the preservation of my work. They said that they no longer had jurisdiction over it in its present state. "And the elbow is unsafe still," they said. "It should be torn down before somebody gets hurt."

Of course I wanted to stand on the elbow—on or in it—with weights and jump up and down to prove that they were wrong. And if it didn't collapse, the work was true. But I felt sure, then, that art would be my downfall and I thought that I and only I would be under the elbow or on it or in it when it collapsed.

In it? Strange that I had not yet gained access to the interior of my own work. I had been asked to enter only that one time and she had not asked me again.

"I want to live inside the elbow." I told her that. She just laughed. "I really do," I said, "and it's more than want. I *need* to be there. But if it has to be that I go in just once, then I'll take only that."

It was just at the moment that I said this that I realized how fearless I'd become. Suddenly I knew I was not afraid of the dark, nor of rats in the dark, nor of overhanging rocks; not afraid of art nor of artists; not afraid of the rich and famous; not afraid of big words nor of long pauses; not afraid to leave the lowest of the locks on my door unlocked; not afraid any longer to wear a weird hat, and not even afraid of Ursula. (Had she goaded me on up to those heights for this very purpose? Was it all a trick to arrive at just this moment when I snatched the keys out of her hand and pushed on and in and past her?)

No sooner had I got inside than she made me feel as if I'd done something wrong. "Not yet," she said, "not yet." "It's a mess," she said, and, "I'm not ready."

The room was like any other living room . . . a lot of antiques, but they looked like they'd been found on the street. Nothing about it even suggested that it was the inside of a statue. For a moment I thought that I and all of my group had been wrong. It wasn't a statue after all. Indeed, it *was* but a row of mismatched huts. The arrangement of the interior made that all the more clear. I had hoped to run around *inside* the breasts, sometime when Ursula wasn't looking, but there was nothing here suggestive of such places. Just two alcoves side by side—one a kitchen, one a breakfast nook. For a moment I had in mind to spend a little time in each, but I wasn't in the mood for that now. "Elbow!" I shouted. She pointed up and said again, "Not yet." But I saw the stairway and pushed past her. This time she *really* tried to stop me, but I was too quick. "No," she shouted, but I was halfway to the top, my head already in the upper room, which was lit by the soft and blue, blue glow of the round eye-windows. But it, too, was just a room-shaped room and like any other attic. There was dust, old boxes, two old trunks . . . but in the corner I saw a ladder that I knew must go to the elbow. And I thought that, if there was, indeed, an elbow, then this must be the statue of a woman as I hoped it was and feared it wasn't, but no longer feared, for if it was a woman then chances were it also might be art.

But now she really didn't want me to go on. She fought desperately. She knocked me down . . . tripped me. And the more we fought, the more desirable became the inside of the elbow. It was as if that had been my goal from the very start. As if it was the only thing I ever really wanted. And I used all my strength against her. She was strong . . . surprisingly strong for one so thin and pale, but at last I threw her from me, making her tear my sleeve right off at the shoulder. She sat there with it dangling in the dust by her knee, looking up at me as I climbed the rickety ladder.

Everything wobbled. The ladder had several missing rungs. One came off as I stepped on it. Some just hung there by one nail, but I got up anyway. Nothing there but a rickety platform. Perhaps it was the danger that had made her want to stop me. Perhaps she was afraid for my safety. Maybe she cared about me and that was why she fought so hard. But now she was coming up after me. The platform was hardly big enough for one, and the whole thing was shaking even more than before and I knew the Landmarks Commission was right, it might fall at any moment. "I'm scared," she said, but she kept climbing. "So am I," I said, as she fell into my arms. And I could not then distinguish my own trembling from her trembling or from the trembling of the platform and of the whole elbow.

By then we were both streaked with grime and our clothes were torn and rumpled. She looked more like the waif she had been—her hair mussed, her stockings ruined, her shoes . . . her high-heeled shoes down on some lower floor. I loved her better like this. I realized it then. I loved her like she used to be . . . like herself.

There was just barely room for us up there, side by side, and I held her so that she wouldn't fall off. The elbow rocked and shivered more and more and I think she'd said yes, just once, instead of no. But just exactly then there came a great crash and shortly after that another. The whole building shook and groaned. My first thought was that we had made the statue come alive, we two, together. My work of art was standing up and taking her elbow from behind her head . . . my statue down the street and out, who knows where? Splinters flew. Beams broke and sagged. It . . . she was walking, and every step was a great crackling. But by the fifth or sixth crash, I knew what was happening. It was the wrecking ball come to demolish the thing before somebody got hurt. A great gap had already parted right in front of us. We tumbled out, half naked, from the hole as the elbow sagged slowly to the ground. The wrecking ball, swinging above our heads, just missed us as we fell. We landed in a forsythia bush (in bloom!).

We laughed because we still held each other. We laughed because we were only scratched and bruised and because the wrecking ball had not quite grazed our heads, and we turned and laughed (because what else was there to do?) to see the whole thing go down flat . . . all shards, even the blue, blue eyes.

Then, still laughing, I pursued her through the bushes of the park. I flushed her from behind trees. I grabbed her and I let her go and she let herself be grabbed again. "Not yet," she said, "not yet," but I pushed on and on, no longer for the sake of women, no longer for the sake of art. Giggling. Giggling. Not for any reason I could think of at the time.

Being Mysterious Strangers from Distant Shores

THEY HAVE BEEN TALKING about a journey into the interior. They know the dangers and yet already they have decided upon it. No one can talk them out of it. It is clear that their minds are made up. Their knapsacks are packed. Their guides have been chosen. They remain cool to suggestions. They smile enigmatic smiles. They no longer answer any questions.

Up to now they have been behaving as tourists should — playing tennis, lying on the beach, eating well, their real lives waiting for them somewhere else. But each of them has yearned to take a trip like this one once in their lives, and they want it now, before they're too old for it. They're still capable even though their median age is fifty-four. Each one thinks he or she can still hike for long hours, can still stand the heat or the cold, can sleep on the ground. There's the tall, fat one and the short, thin one (soon to be fast friends). There's a man who hopes to find gold. There's a woman who is going along as a protest against the government's tax policies. She plans not to pay taxes while she is in the interior. There's a man who will not stand by passively and let millions die of starvation in a well-known African country. He plans to donate one dollar for each mile covered by every person who returns safely. He will keep track of the mileage on his pedometer, and will not be distressed if there are several false starts or doublings back. There is the man who has chosen the journey instead of committing suicide and there is the woman who has chosen the journey in order to feel more alive. There is one who is going along because he is concerned about the civil rights of all the small brown men with black bangs of the world (and women, too) and on this journey he hopes to encounter some of them. And then there is the failed politician, the failed lawyer, the failed doctor, and the failed psychologist. The latter had hoped to get some kind of grant to study what kinds of people go on journeys such as this and how they behave under the stresses of such journeys, but the money was not forthcoming (as is usual in his case). He is not discouraged by that and is going along anyway and hopes to write a book about it that will sell well. His preliminary studies have shown that the tourists going on the journey are not statistically different from those tourists who are not going on the journey. This is disappointing; however, he hopes to prove that those coming back will have been significantly changed.

For a few of them the journey may be considered as the moral equivalent of something much more violent.

The dangers of the interior must be many, because they have found only three guides willing to go with them: small brown men with black bangs and long knives. Two of these men say they have been halfway into the interior and one says he has been all the way. The adventurers don't know whether to believe them or not. Some think the guides have never been farther than the outskirts of town. Others say that they may be, on the other hand, themselves from the interior; that they know all about it; that this is a trap and that they have been sent out from the interior expressly for the purpose of guiding unsuspecting tourists like themselves back into it, for purposes that no one can imagine but that might well be nefarious. Still others think they're just ignorant peasant-types who want the money and probably will run off with all the rifles, cameras, and hiking boots, leaving the adventurers stranded halfway to the interior and halfway from civilization.

This only makes the tourists all the more excited about going. No way of telling what dangers and adventures await them. They are well aware that some of their number may not return. Some may die and some may want to become permanent residents of the interior, and yet they are all confident that some of them will return. After all, they are so many. And each one thinks, thought he is hardly aware of it, that he will be among those who will return. And each one hopes, though he is hardly aware of it, that he will find his heart's desire or—and better yet—find something totally unexpected he didn't even know he yearned for. Some think perhaps it will be spiritual, as though they were going to India instead. The man searching for gold hopes he will return with a completely unforeseen sort of treasure. The tall fat man expects not only to become thin, but to become something better than just thinner. The man who is going along instead of committing suicide thinks (and this is such a tiny thought that he is completely unaware of it) that perhaps he will find a reason for living. He thinks he's too young to die. He's fifty-one and a runner, and having watched his diet carefully for several years, he feels he's in better shape than most much younger men, and often says so. Still, his eyes are sad. When he is walking along the beach he thinks of swimming out into the ocean and not coming back, though this is not an uncommon thought of many far less suicidal people.

None of these people knew each other before, though some had friends of friends in common. Several first met in the lobby of the Hilton. Six or seven got together and then the word spread. Those who wanted or needed to hear about the journey seemed to hear about it, many in mysterious ways, as: one was told of it by a wizened old man in a souvenir shop full of strange carvings said to have been done by natives of the interior. Another was told by the swimming instructor. One even heard of it in a letter from the States, though how or why word could have reached the States is certainly a matter for conjecture.

Now all sixty-seven of them are walking through the brush in the direction that they have presumed the interior to be (aided, of course, in this decision by their three guides). And the man for whom this trip is to be considered a form of suicide (regardless of what his unconscious motives may be) has already teamed up with the woman who is taking the trip in order to feel more alive.

Though they are well underway, they will all have to hurry if they want to reach the interior before the rainy season.

They are a colorful lot, still dressed more or less as tourists since they didn't have time to get completely outfitted — and also many of them feel they don't want to invest in expensive new olive-drab jungle clothes and camouflage jump suits. So they are wearing shirts as bright as the jungle flowers around them, and white slacks, white sneakers, or red or blue striped running shoes (though many already had olive-drab jungle clothes and camouflage jump suits). After the first few hours of the journey, the white things become smudged, probably permanently. In spite of this, the idea that many unforeseen — and perhaps even some very startling things —

can happen at any time, has kept them in a light-hearted mood. They are singing and whistling along the way.

But there's also a lovers' reasons for their gaiety. Those who are single hope to find partners and those who are still married hope for a resurgence of the romantic feelings of their honeymoons, though some, it's true, are hoping to be able to swap mates with other couples, if only temporarily. They all hope, however, to avoid emotionally draining scenes. In short, and in spite of their ages, they are a troupe of lovers, or possible lovers. None wants to make do with love as it's been so far. They believe all their former ways of loving have been merely practice phases they had to go through in order to reach some new and higher point. Why can't I, each one is thinking, have a love at least as grand as the loves I've read about or seen on TV? Am I so different from those lucky ones? And so they sing.

It is to be hoped that all their quarrels will be lovers' quarrels.

Their progress is slow as they stop to admire the tropical foliage and listen to the birds. The man with the pedometer is constantly urging them on in hopes of increasing their mileage. They are all (for their ages) in very good shape, as previously mentioned, what with the tennis, swimming, skiing, etc., they've been doing during their weekends and vacations. But, though they're used to the exercise, they're not so used to sleeping on the ground. Also, as older people, their bursitis bothers them and they get stiff necks. In a few days, lack of sleep makes them irritable, but most are trying hard to make the journey a positive experience, knowing that it will be, as the psychologist has reiterated, largely what they themselves make of it. Suffice it to say that they proceed without grave incidents and with only minor annoyances and injuries across the low lands and soon they begin their ascent into the mountains they must cross in order to reach the interior.

Mary, for that is the name of the woman hoping to feel more alive, is quite pleased with the adventure. "If," she said, "if the adventure is nothing more than what it has proved to be so far, I will be satisfied with it."

Think of Australia with its bull-roarers, kangaroo tail roasts, dijeridoos, bolos, boomerangs, and black-skinned but blonde children. The adventurers hope to find people and artifacts no less strange, men with mysteries of their own so that matches will not surprise them at all. Still, the adventurers hope to be able to give medical advice and to tell them about civilized ways in general, and that it is dangerous for children to play with bees on the end of a string as some of them saw once in a picture in an old *National Geographic*.

Some adventurers even hope they will find savage little black or brown lovers coming together in what might, at first, be taken for lewd and random couplings but that wouldn't be, and that the adventurers might learn a few new tricks.

It is on the ascent that the cheerful (in spite of having failed) little psychologist really makes himself known. Though small and no younger than any of the others, he is very strong and runs up and down the mountain paths urging them on to do and risk and be. At night he listens to the rundown of their aches and pains and presides over sensory awareness exercises for those who want them, and in the mornings he analyzes their dreams. He had them all sized up from the beginning, of course: the border-line, the narcissistic, the passive-aggressive, the hysteric. He would like to discourage unrealistic expectations. He will, of course, be confining himself to neutral interventions and he hopes not to provide any inappropriate gratification.

They have no sooner gotten into some really hard climbing than it becomes clear that one of their number suffers from a real psychosis. He stands on the edge of a precipice threatening to throw himself over. At first he mumbles and gesticulates in a way that no one understands, not even the cheerful psychologist; but now he's speaking quite rationally.

"All I ever wanted was a little love," he says. "Not a lot. Just a little bit of love and glory. It's all my wife's fault. If I jump, you can blame her for it. All I ever wanted was to be a part of something beautiful." (It is clear that he too can be counted among the lovers.)

"You're just overtired," his wife says. She tells the others not to worry. That she's used to this. Their names are Henry and Margaret.

Jack, for that is the name of the previous suicidal man, tells Mary that he, on the other hand, is not impressed by either beauty or love. Sensory pleasures mean nothing to him. All the world, whether at sunset or midnight, looks equally gray to him. He himself would hardly bother to jump. Being dead or alive, what difference does it make? What he says is not entirely true, though it does make Mary very sad. She wants to help him. Of course she, like the rest of the women, is a little old to be really desirable even (or especially) to an older man, but she has hopes, and always tries to keep her white shorts spotless, or at least less smudged than those of the others. (So far there has not been a dearth of streams to wash in, though that changes now. In fact, they are no sooner adjusted to life in the jungle than they must adjust to life above the timberline.)

Later on, Jack's touch will make her blood run wild.

Like the psychologist the failed doctor has also been a great help. He has brought along a knapsack full of drugs, mostly for himself, but he's not unwilling to share them with others in times of great need or even not great need. Once they spent the whole evening, tired as they were, giggling at nothing.

Suddenly there's a frantic yell from one of their number far ahead and higher up. The yell echoes. Hard to tell which is the real yell or where it's coming from. There is the clump and bounce of falling rocks. Unfortunately, the person who, at this very moment, is falling to his death is not Henry, the man who wanted to jump a few hours before. The body, which comes to rest on the rocks far below — a mere dot, one needs field glasses to make out that the yellow is the hat and the red the backpack — certainly must be a sobering view to Henry. He is probably glad, now, that he didn't jump.

Later that night, as they are camped precariously in the hollow of a huge cirque, they are wondering: Has he died in vain? For no good cause at all? They would like to think not. They vote (unanimously) to continue the journey in his name. To turn back now, or at any point along the way, would negate all he had suffered. Which of us was he, anyway, they ask each other. Many thought it was the Frenchman, but he is still here. Some thought it was the lawyer or the fat man, but they're here also. The doctor is still here. Soon they begin to wonder if the cry was that of a man or a woman. There is a great deal of argument. Finally, they vote to go on in memory of the unknown person, whether male or female, and agree that the journey itself should serve as a memorial and that it be conducted in the spirit of love of the wilderness which he or she certainly must have felt or how could he or she have brought himself/herself to come on such a trip in the first place? And so it is resolved that they continue in memory of this unknown person.

That night there are several hailstorms as though the very heavens were mourning the death of that man or woman. The adventurers huddle together for warmth and protection, crouching in the lee of boulders trying to protect their heads. All their hats, without exception, are ruined.

In the morning as they top the edge of the col, they wonder if they are dreaming. Is this a flight of fancy? What they see before them seems a paradise. It's one of those fairly high valleys, green and wooded with streams and even a lake. They are all thinking it's too bad that whoever it was that fell their death couldn't be here now to see it. They decide to descend to the place and spend the next day or so resting up and repairing their gear and clothes. Surely there are small animals and fish. Perhaps even deer. They will eat well and sleep on moss or, better yet, beds of ferns. (From the look of it, the interior itself cannot be far off.)

But this is not to be.

They do descend into that disappointing valley, but it is soon clear that this is neither the happy valley they expect nor the outskirts of the interior at last. They are conjecturing that perhaps there is a black (or white) queen who has had advance news of all their actions so far. She has silenced her drums and hidden the thatch of her palaces, driven away the animals, dammed up her streams, leaving only a few crawdads for the adventurers to eat.

Even so, steadfastly, they push on, beyond this valley, through forests, over cliffs, across plains . . . now and then sensing a mysterious presence beyond the trees, sure (or almost sure) that they are being watched: rustlings, phoney bird calls (or so they think), the snap of twigs . . . at night the sound of whispering when all of them are, supposedly, asleep.

And now they are losing two or three of their numbers at almost every ascent or descent. Though, it is true, two of them just seemed to dwindle away. Both women. They did not complain, but it was clear that they were not overwhelmed by the grandeur of *any* of the views. (One might presume they had not found anyone to love them.)

"Had they only been willing to talk to me," the psychologist says on numerous occasions after they die, although (as is well known) no one can ever make anyone else go for help.

When they do, at last, come to that particular vast fertile plain which they all take to be interior itself— and they hope the end of their journey — they arrive minutes too late. The fires are still warm and smoking, some with pots still full of hot stew (for that small favor the adventurers are grateful). But of what use is such a journey when the interior retreats before them in this fashion, one valley, one forest, one cliff at a time, the residents carrying away the structural supports of all the houses so that the roofs collapse or, as in the former valley, leaving nothing at all? What use, when nothing is left of statues but their niches; and no banners, only the poles they flew from? But perhaps if they hurry they can catch up with the interior before it recedes altogether. And so, in spite of everything, they push on with renewed vigor and hope.

They are feeling now that if they all should die soon — and even though they still know very little about the true interior — they will certainly no longer die in complete ignorance of it.

Were one to undertake some such journey one's self, one could certainly expect to be greatly changed by it. One might establish whole sets of new values — come to new conclusions. One would certainly hope to find (even if only a few) definitive answers to questions of the universe as well as to universal questions, though one might not be able to make the necessary changes in one's own life even so. One can but wonder if this has happened — new answers, that is — to any of the adventurers as they push on with renewed hope.

But perhaps it could be said that their very hopes are deceiving them. If only they could stop hoping they might come to some reasonable conclusions and act in accordance with them. At their age, most of their false expectations should have fallen by the wayside, but it seems this hasn't happened. It is clear that not a single one of them will turn back even after the next set of hardships. (Vast fertile plains can have problems, too, including mosquitoes, snakes, and leeches.) Always around the next corner, they will be thinking — or after the next mile, or one more day — something will happen . . . something will turn up.

It is to be hoped that it is not the fear of looking ridiculous that keeps them going.

Let them go. The best is not to be, anyway, neither here nor there, whatever their illusions. Even so, one wishes the best for them. That they should lie down (exhausted in the dark) next to some old grass shack and wake up on the outskirts of a city of a thousand temples. Or that they should fall (exhausted in the dark) on the sands of a drab beach and wake up to a thousand ships in a sparkling bay. Or that they should sleep (exhausted in the dark) next to what seems like only a large square stone and yet wake up to a thousand ornate plinths in long rows, each one larger than the one before, and upon each, the golden feet of the statues that once stood there . . . .

But what of Mary and Jack? Suffice it to say that his touch has already made her blood run wild.

And now the rainy season will begin.

As If

WE WERE SINGLED OUT, rounded up, subjected to scrutiny, confined to such spaces as seemed (to them) suitable for us. We were accused of being mere imitations, but how tell a good imitation from the real thing? We ourselves don't know, or hardly know, or didn't know then, but do now, though we're still not sure. They said they had been suspicious all along, and actually, we also have always had suspicions about ourselves. However, we revealed to them the selves we have, for some time now, tried to be. We didn't tell them that we hardly knew what they were talking about — that we only dimly sensed (then) the rightness of what they said. We had by that time forgotten what was true and what was false, even though we have always known that we are false in many ways in spite of our strivings — or perhaps because of our strivings — to be ourselves: as why should we have to work so hard to be who we "really" are if we really are it? And yet our smiles have always seemed to genuine, even (or especially) to ourselves.

We believe that no beings of our caliber have ever been taken before — none quite so "equal-to," so rosy and lucent, so (at times) outwardly serene — our capacity for suffering only equal to our capacity for joy. (But this last is such a truism as to be hardly worth the words to say it.)

They used dogs to sniff us out, not trusting themselves to be sure of our differences. Even our own pets sensed that we didn't belong.

The day of our capture, it was perfect weather for intellectuals.

Only that once we appeared before them topless (we are pleased with our appearance), but this didn't change their attitude though we hoped it might. (We had, by that time, been unjustly accused of having come from other planets.)

We kept our answers to a minimum because we didn't understand their questions. Usually we talk a lot because we are also pleased with our language and proud of it. It's the one with the most words, and good ones too, such as *aquatint, fudge,* and *quilt;* and phrases such as *hitch it to*, and *Ed edited it* and *Bob'll be back*. Then there's endings like *fists, ghosts, risks,* and so on. What could be more fun! So we talk.

We have been captured along with many of our artifacts: parasols, chiffonniers, love seats, lap desks, shuttlecocks . . . a miscellany of what we consider poetry but they do not, also art that we consider art and they, etc. They say none of our arts make any sense at all.

"Why other planets?" we ask.

They're acting as if it's our own fault that we have been accused of this. We look so much like them, too. One of us looks like a well-known movie star and one looks like a long-dead author (and dresses the part in purple velvet), and one looks like Wanda Landowska, and two look like versions of the young Frank Sinatra, while another looks like the elderly version. Four look like Joyce Carol Oates.

It seems we have done such a good job at pretending, that we have kept ourselves secret even from ourselves. I was unaware that all these others (and I was even unaware that I myself) were "us" until we were confined here in this unsuitable place. We have kept up this masquerade for so long that we wonder if there's any hope of recovering even small bits of who we really are under the debris accumulated while pretending to be "them." If we fail to find ourselves, we will be condemned to being "them" even if they continue to accuse us of being alien, saying our eyes are too this or that; our hair, our noses, too much or not enough; and so forth.

It was only after I was rounded up as one of "us" (picked out by my own Pomeranian) that I began to remember that I had once asked myself all the same questions they are asking us: Who was I? Where had I come from? Where *had* I come from! The explanations I had received—we all had received—were too ridiculous to be taken seriously. First there were those stories of being found under a mushroom, but then our mothers took us aside for a serious talk and told us the outrageous business with two sexes—a tale more outlandish than the one about the storks. This only made us wonder all the more what the real story could be. (That we come from other planets doesn't seem unreasonable by comparison.) None of us felt that any of this had much to do with us. Certainly I knew it had nothing to do with me—even (or especially) the fact that I was one sex and not the other, and had had no choice in the matter. And why two sexes anyway? And why did I have to be one of them?

Then there were those two people, so unlike me, from whom I was accused of descending. No one told the truth, not even others of my own age. They giggled and whispered and told "under-a-sheet" jokes. False. Even the jokes. I knew that at the time. At least I knew it was false for me. All of "us" knew that.

We thought we'd learn the real story when we were old enough, but we never seemed to get old enough, and then we got used to things as they seemed to be and I and we kept on pretending we were like everybody else, did what was expected of us, dressed like them, talked like them. What else was there to do? We had no other models. Besides, we were afraid of who we were. We hardly dared to think about ourselves at all sometimes, especially as we grew older, for fear of what we might find out.

We all remember it like this, but now we are trying to think back . . . back to before we had been given so many wrong answers — right for "them" but wrong for "us" — back to when we were saying: How come all these bridges, and Eiffel Towers (two of them now!), and clothes? Back to when we were laughing at shoes and umbrellas.

Our captors are right. We must have come from other planets. And, as we live here now, confined to this space, our differences from "them" become more and more clear. We actually *are* "we" and they are clearly "they." Take our names, for instance. We are Rhodanthe, Leatrice, Alastair, Diamanta, Celandine, Ethelbert, Zipporah, Odelette . . . . The guards' names, on the other hand, are Jim, Ben, Sue, Don, Bill, Tom, etc. They are, clearly, not from the same world as we.

We've had little luck remembering our planet. "Airy," someone said. "Free," another. "No clothes, of course. No clothes needed." "No higher values. No higher values needed." "Or at least we never talked about them" "Or perhaps that's all we talked about." "In any case, we were always good. No morals, therefore. No morals needed." "No rain." "Yes, rain. It's needed." "No, no rain except in the mountains. It rolls down to the valleys. It covers the plains with just the right amount of water. Poppies bloom."

"Earth men," we say, and often, "we must have come in peace. As far as we can tell, we must have come in peace, bearing gifts of technological advances which we have forgotten and are, therefore, unable to give to you at the present time." (Surely we must have come with plans for a better and fairer life than this one is.)

The guards stare at us in strange ways; hostile, but also as if admiring, and in truth, there is much to admire. Perhaps they are falling in love. They are cruel, but that may also be a sign of their love. There are strange electricities that pass between us.

Our prison is large, a palace of a prison: high, rounded ceiling, tall windows, mirrors. Small birds, nesting atop its pilasters add their tweets to our songs. It's so large that even with all of us here, standing around in little groups of four or five, there's plenty of room. Perhaps this is deliberate on their part. Perhaps this great hall is meant to suggest outer space and we, as we stand here, clusters of planetary systems. Perhaps they hope this will help us to remember. We play their game. We circle in planetary ways. We sing in thirds, fifths, and octaves—music of the spheres. (We have high, sweet voices.) When we dance, and we often do dance, it is in stately imitation of what goes on in the heavens, though as it gets later in the night, after only the young are left, the dances change—degenerate, some would way—to wild imitations of punk and rock. *Good* imitations, as with everything we do.

I am young. Am I young? They've kept telling me my age all along, but I never did believe them any more than I believe any of the other things they say. I can feel how young I am—slim and willowy. I think young thoughts. I dance when the young dance. I'm so young as to know only as much as the young know.

There is one particular guard who watches me. (Why would he bother if I were old?) I never look at him. I flow, twirl, I flap my long, cold hands. I pretend to play the spinet. (I'm the one who looks like Wanda Landowska.)

We hear rumors that there will soon be torture, but we have already confessed—have confessed, in fact, from the start, before we were sure of anything, before we understood what they were asking. "Guilty," we said, "whatever the charges." We've often felt we shouldn't be here on this earth, we should be somewhere else or never born, if, indeed, we *were* born. (To ourselves, we simply appeared. "I am here," we said, looking in the mirror.)

But they are saying that torture will help us to remember. They say it's for our own good. They say we will, at last, know ourselves as we want to know ourselves. So when that particular guard takes me to a side room, I am forewarned. I don't expect it to have anything to do with love. (Though who can guess what "love" means to any other creature? I don't even know what *I* mean by it.) But why did he pick me? Did I give some unconscious, secret signal?

He is a wide man (not fat) with soft, practiced hands. When he's finished there won't be a mark on me. I'm thinking he would make a good lover, knowing what he does about the hidden places for pain.

He doesn't accept any of my answers. I had, even before, wondered what sort of Bach-like planet Wanda Landowska would have come from: water flowing with the sound of triplets, three giraffes against four white hillocks, two moons, the whole sky twinkling like the music does. But the guard keeps saying no until I get so tired my mind works in a different way, and I see he was right to go on like this. Now I do know—or at least my mouth knows. "Outer space is sweet," I hear myself say, "and full of dust. It glitters. My head aches at the thought of it."

"True," he says, and takes his thumb from my wrist bone.

We have been through a lot together by now. Do we love each other? The torture has been with such sweet, slow passion. He has even said "My love" though as if inadvertently . . . absentmindedly.

But now he has put his thumb back on my wrist and his other thumb at my elbow. His left foot is poised over my instep. He holds the long end of my scarf in his teeth as though to cut short my next words. I speak quickly. I tell myself to stick to the stars as they are perceived by "them." "We floated for centuries in the glimmer of space," I say, "always as young as we are at this very moment." But the torture has already begun again.

They always say to live in the present, but I want to be free of that tyranny. I will skip the now. I will move on to another time before now can catch me up in it. I will levitate into the future. I am already dizzy with acrophobia. But I have to fill in these few seconds of the now while I take the jump beyond them. I have to keep talking. "This world," I say, and I have already said it, "in what other world than this one would the moon be as this moon is and the sun as this sun, and clouds, sunsets, dew, smoke, oceans . . . ."

He pulls the scarf tight—has already pulled it. He has already said, "My dear, dear lady."

If I could have spoken, I would have said, "I love you just as if I really loved you," but I can only sputter. Then suddenly, he lets my green gauze go. Perhaps he can see I'm not in the now anymore. He lets go of me completely and I fall at his feet, nothing left of me to hold myself up by. I'm as if fit only for a watery world. Perhaps that's it: water world! But I can hardly speak.

Has this, then, already been the final moment between us? (He has lifted me up. He has held me in a lover's grip, one hand on my breast.) I wanted to make the moment last. I wanted to be in it, but it eluded me. I lived in the future instead. I was already back here, surrounded by mirrors and by "us." I hardly noticed that he held me before he had already dropped me in the middle of the great hall. Without his powerful arms about me and one hand on my breast, without the bristles of his beard against my cheek, without his rapt . . . enraptured attention, I'm but a rag — a sweaty, panting thing — imitation of a thing. I lie here being me only as if me, the birds as if birds (tweeting and swooping), my gauzy scarf as if wings.

But no. A change. "Look!" I manage to croak it out. "The real me, and yet — imagine that — only a little different from the way I was before!" I'm thinking one tiny change can go a long way, but he's already down the hall, traveling at the speed of time. It's too late to call him back. It's too late to tell him I'm believing what "they" tell me as fast as I can.

Slowly Bumbling in the Void

THERE IS A NEED in all of us to build a little house, log by log or stone by stone. There is a need to sew up a little mattress for the floor, to stash away dried food in leather pouches (rice and figs); a need to make a little set of shelves and to put up a hook for our coat and another hook for our pan. There is a need to make soup out of old bones, to gather dandelion greens and prepare them according to a grandmother's recipe. Then there is a need that a storm should rage outside and that we should sleep through it. Afterwards — after, that is, the need to make a map of the territory — there is a need in all of us to move in time to some kind of tapping, to move (decorated and with hat) to tunes or to play a game with small stones, and all the while, to be on the lookout for something mysterious.

There is a need in me to knit a scarf for you, to make (for you) an overcoat out of a blanket. There is a need to string a wire from the telephone to the pole in order to call you up. There is a need for a calendar of the coming year in order to write down what will happen in the future and in order to mark an X on the days when you will be here. There is a need for a little alarm clock and perhaps a little wind-up toy that hops and turns in circles with a clicking sound. (These are for you.)

I also want to prepare for you a fish that you caught with your bare hands in my stream. I need to prepare your fish. I need to hear you call me by my name holding out your fish.

"I said I want to cook your fish! Were you listening to me then? Are you listening to me now?"

He isn't listening.

He has a funny shape for a hero, but then I have never been known as a full-breasted woman.

It's still the simple life — except now, to go anywhere, one always needs keys and a watch.
Speak of the hero before he appears (under the black, ceremonial umbrella) saying: These are the beloved's dark brown socks. (Your socks.) Here, his dirty shirt. It is his hairs that are stuck in the comb. This is where he spilled his drink. This is where he put his fist through the wall saying, "We must find a peaceful solution to our marriage." But he has put his cheek against my birthmark. He has licked lint from my navel. He has washed my feet.

But already it's several years later and we have moved on now into a whole other category. You've turned the cottage into a TV station or it might as well be. I'm not the star here even though I'm blinded by lights that are reflected in the surfaces of utensils and mirrors that belong to both of us. My blemishes are revealed and catalogued and held against me. "Oh." I say it for the camera. "Oh wind, sand, and dim (suburban) stars . . . vast plain with here and there a ridiculous promontory . . ." (It's Long Island. New York is on the horizon. Perhaps life would be better here if it were the other way around.)

So how do I look on my way to the waterfall, especially now that it's several years later? Still shrouded in mystery? Still seen as though from behind a scrim of desire? Though how long can a scrim like that last? Look. This is me leaning over to drink from the water. This is me taking off one shoe and putting my foot in even though it's ice-cold. This is you, happening to notice my foot. I believe I have revealed another blemish.

But how begin to describe myself even to myself? How do it when caught suddenly between short hair and long? Between the big middle period of life and old age? Between one kind of love and the next higher form? Another day, in other words, and a whole other category of existence in which I may even make a move in the direction of freedom . . . freedom, that is, around a fixed point. (You.)

But he has turned away already, crying out, "Direct access," (a not unfamiliar cry where the media is concerned) or is it, "Direct success"?

How make love grow? (There is a need.) (There is a responsibility.) Proceed along given lines set forth in certain books. (It's already an exact science.) Don't wait to be asked! Keep both hands busy at the same time. Mouth. He may be grateful. (I kissed his instep.)

In your dream you were proud of your enormous penis. You showed if off to me, suspecting I wouldn't like it, and you were right, I didn't, even in your dream. In my dream the vagina stuck out like a duck's beak and snapped up everything it could reach. In your dream you puffed yourself up still further until it would have taken some giantess to engulf you. In my dream it wasn't a question of size, but that the vicious vagina could snap off your hand if you reached for me. In answer to my dream you dreamt your giant penis tore me in two. In my next dream you went limp all of a sudden (probably from some remark of mine) and had to stuff your long, weak self down your left pant leg and on into your shoe.

He wants to take good care of his penis.
He wants to make good use of it.

There is a need in me to make a gesture in the direction of freedom, outwards from a fixed point which is you. There is a need to project an upward climb and to make promises (if only to myself) and to make, also, a little chart for the wall in order to keep track of the progress. Freedom is up the left side. Love is marked along the bottom line. No, I mean time, in increments of half a day, along the bottom. Progress is inevitably outwards, therefore, from the fixed point of what we used to be to each other. There may be happy accidents. One can look forward to them. A complete new repertoire of behavior may be possible for both of us, including reversal of roles, dancing, rage, and even mediocrity. (I have sometimes, here on this featureless plain, made myself bland out of the fear of being bland.)

Up to now, we have been leading a kind of once-over-lightly life.

Here on this plain, New York on the horizon, futile rustic gestures in the form of tree-lined streets, you have offered me cookies. These are the cookies of love. (This is in a dream.) I laugh behind my hand

and only pretend to be delighted. I don't dare take any and I act out an enthusiasm for them that I do not feel. Why, in this dream, do I not allow myself to take them? Why, in this dream, do I want to laugh at you?

Even so, I give you the run of my little house, but you want more headroom.

Reality appears in the form of a long journey. You have gone to the mountainous region in search of direct access and a hands-on experience though you have professed to be in search of semiprecious stones.

You yourself become the missing element.

You are no longer under the ceremonial black umbrella.

I wear a monkey's skull on the other end of my tether. (It's for show. I have tied it there myself.)

A hundred years ago this land was marshlands. It's no wonder, then, that all roads become impassable, and that I can't even make my way to my own kitchen where I had hoped to conduct experiments (culinary) on your fist. I mean, fish. (It has crawled away gasping. I heard it in the middle of the night) I will call you up. (Assuming, that is, that I can make it to the phone.) I want to tell you something that's not a defense or a pretense or an explanation.

At this moment I yearn to reinvent the wheel (heating damp wood until it can be forced to form a circle), making a light, quick vehicle for myself. I want to reinvent it slowly, one step at a time; first as a toy, later on in a bicycle, then a VW, skipping the ox cart altogether or anything ponderous. But I hardly get started before you return of your own accord, having tied your fig leaf back on the tree. You are humming. "Come share an intimate moment with me and the camera," you are saying. You order more film and a drum and a flute and a basket of feathers. This reunion is a once-in-a-lifetime opportunity. The possibility of muffing it makes you (or so you tell me) feel as if you are adrift in a small, un-seaworthy boat. Perhaps you have, in the hiatus, become a poet of sorts. The children (there actually are children by now) are told not to expect too much from Daddy and Mommy in the next few days. The title of your new work will be *See the Lovers Still Attacked*. I know you mean *Attached . . . Still Attached*. You missed it by only one letter.

We hollow out a log in order to see what sort of musical instrument will result. Then we will move, decorated and with hats.

I see by the chart on our wall that we have moved on up into another category. The tan line, which was followed for a short time by a sort of ugly grayish-green line, is now followed by the beginnings of a more or less blue line. There is an infinitesimal, but clearly perceptible, upward swing. We are also one full square outwards. Love is along the top and to be aimed for. Time, at a quarter of an inch for half a day, is along the bottom. Freedom (a subdivision of space) is outwards from a fixed point. (You.)

Escape Is No Accident

I HEAR MYSELF making a sound like an animal.

I come to slowly.

Dizzy.

Having fallen out of the sky.

Crashed here at two o'clock Eastern Standard time.

No hope of rescue.

But I'm already hoping.

Certain I must have landed in or near New York because my first view was of, yes, blue eyes and beard. I didn't recognize him. Lying back in his arms, I was wondering who he was.

He warmed me the best way he could, with his own body stretched out next to mine, and all the while making soft word-sounds I couldn't understand.

He guessed who I was.

I never did.

Later on he carried me inside and dressed my wounds. I was a mass of cuts and bruises, and childlike at the time.

He always says *he* didn't do it and I never said he did.

I know it's my fault. I came in much too fast. I always do and I think I had a dizzy spell even before. I had passed all the tests devised for it so far, but I know I wasn't up to my usual standards and maybe I shouldn't have tried, but I wanted, just this once, to cross the celestial equator by myself and send back messages of grandeur, hope and good luck, though it isn't every morning you face yourself, plucking out gray hairs and sweating, knowing your reflexes are shot—which is maybe another reason why I missed the night side and landed, two o'clock, on the opposite continent right in my own backyard. Or so *he* says.

"Me, husband." Pointing to himself. "Uh, uh."

"What am I doing crash-landed here in my own backyard?" I ask, but he doesn't understand me anymore than I can understand him.

"You, wife. Yeah."

Under the circumstances I feel vaguely as if I had fallen off a ladder while painting the upstairs window sills, but that can't be.

"Me from sky," I say, pointing up. "We got messages. We got the picture with one of each sex, man and woman, and a sun. We understood all that. That's why I'm here."

"Yeah, I get it. Sex and that."

How many days did I lie there in his bed, semiconscious, feverish and frightened, waking up screaming sometimes, not knowing who I was and my husband—his hairy arms around me—comforting me? How many days drifting up from sickness and back, his hand on my breast?

"What day is this? What time? What place? I hardly recognize it."

"Me, husband. Uh . . . listen, we call this here, *pan*; this, *potholder*, *spoon*, *mop* an' stuff."

I think he expects something of me now that I'm fully recovered, but I feel I need a long rest and I had hoped, wherever I might be, to have a fairly creative career, and actually, every time I fell asleep lately I was hoping to wake up someplace else entirely.

"Hey, you. . . ."

"I object," I tell him. "I'd much rather have some sort of teaching position. I'm a member of the association for the advancement of cognitive thinking. I'm aware of the new studies of the sensory and perceptual processes and I speak a number of languages that not a single person on this planet can possibly know but me, not to mention that fact that I'm a fully trained astronomer. Besides, you should take me to your leader."

He says he hasn't had much time to learn things. I think I hurt his pride or his feelings and I'd really like to make up for it somehow. "Well," I tell him, "I'll have to think this out, and in the meantime, I may as well make some spaghetti."

He tells me that would be nice and not to forget to make enough for the children, but he doesn't say how many there are or give ages and sexes or if I can expect any of them to help me with the dishes.

He says, "Shape up."

It turns out today is Tuesday. Never a very good day on any celestial body.

"There's not only just one way to be a good wife, you know," I tell him. "Besides, where I come from we usually live alone. It's expected. We're brought up for it. Mothers always say to daughters, When you grow up and go off alone and don't do what I did, you'll be single and simple and can live as you please."

"Go ahead an' cry. It's OK," he says, and he says he's got money enough for dancing lessons if I like that sort of thing.

I tested him surreptitiously and found him wanting, though I do admire him in several ways. He wakes me with music he whistles himself. He praises my breasts. He listens when I talk even though he doesn't understand much. He worries about me. He lets me have my way sometimes. He taught me lots of different ways for making love and he keeps asking, "Do you love me? Do you love me?" and I never know quite what to answer. I tell him that I know that the butterfly is a symbol of the female sex organs, while the caterpillar, on the other hand, is a symbol of the male. That seems to satisfy him for a little while.

I'll be seeking my fortune behind his back if necessary. I'm going to try to win a trip for two for as far away as I can manage and then take both trips myself consecutively. I may send some bottles into space on tiny rockets with calls for help, one to each of the cardinal directions with a message saying: Remember me, I'm stuck here in this ordinary solar system, ordinary planet, ordinary backyard (though if the fifth planet goes nova it'll be quite an interesting binary system). You may not recognize me. My uniform is torn and has spaghetti on it. I have a constant ringing in my ears. But be careful when you come. You might turn out to be somebody's wife. He says, "Shape up." I want to know if I should bother trying to make him proud of me. I think I'm pregnant and what about all these other children?

A long message, but to the point, and one that will, I hope elicit compassion.

He is Wabb, son of Argg, and I'm drifting into a new role in which I recognize the plight of the overeducated suburban woman being a helpmeet to her hard-working spouse.

But just suppose I really have fallen off a ladder while painting the window sills: Why then would I find their language so full of simple sounds and twangs that leave me cold? I'm exhausted with it. There's hardly a combination of sounds that doesn't mean something to them somewhere.

And even though I heard myself making the cry of an animal (I remember that), still, *they* are the ones that try to understand everything on an instinctual level and get most of it wrong at that.

"Hey, no more sittin' around starin' into space." (I was looking at the sky in hope of rescue.)

"I still think you should take me to your leader."

"Noxin? Don't be silly."

'Tis the season to be jolly. Down at the South Pole the sun's rays slant sideways all day long and night too, or most of it, coming in every window in turn. That's one way to look on the bright side of things, and anyway, you have to trust who you can. After all, I haven't got a cent of their kind of money. What can I do? But speaking of money, if *I* were choosing (and I hope someday I get the chance), I'd bring a better class of people down here who wouldn't always charge what the market will bear.

I tell him it's very likely we will die in an earthquake or tornado. In any case, great winds will come. They will not be man-made. Tides will be higher than ever before. The continents will shrink. Day will be like night. Scientists will scream that the world is tipping and only people with a college degree will be saved.

"Whatta you really want? Beaucoup is too much."

"I would like to be numbered among the survivors and also be on the committee to choose the others that should survive. You might not be one of them."

Meanwhile, I've already called him "darling" twice without thinking what I was saying. Oh, I would have so much preferred a Renaissance man of some sort and one a little less thick at the waist. This morning, though, I thought I saw a faint spark of understanding in his eyes. There may be some hope after all.

I am no ordinary woman. At least I don't *think* so. Sometimes I'm mistaken for a boy and they say I will soon give birth to twins. Not something everyone does. (If I don't command attention, perhaps *they* will soon command respect. For this reason I hope they are both male. Also I would like a couple of little penises to look at when I feel like it.) These twins will not be ordinary babies, and it's true, they're not. Time has gone by so fast that I have given birth to them already and they *are* male, faintly mongoloid, blue . . . but all babies have blue eyes. As soon as they are old enough to call me Muth-uh I'll tell them my own story: That I come from a strange place in the sky, invisible to the naked eye. Something called a planet, where life goes on much as it does here except that the policy-making is left to those who can handle it.

Just then I thought I heard the archetypal man's deep bass voice, but it was only him, Wabb son of Argg, calling the neighbors to celebrate the birth of twins.

It's my unique past, I'll tell them. . . . "It's Muth-uh's unique past that has made her what she is today."

But now *he's* calling me Muth-uh, too. I sputter and try to reply in kind: "Daddy . . . uh . . . duh . . . Da . . . Pop."

"Come to muh big fat arms, ya bastid," he says.

I wish he would enunciate more clearly. I'm not really sure that's what he said at all, but I come anyway. It doesn't matter how close I get because I had garlic for lunch. He puts his arms around me. "Dream girl, yup, take a break now." I feel his big lips below my ear, then down on my neck, and I'm thinking there are a lot of different ways of being sophisticated.

But I believe I have made a tragic mistake. I should have been concentrating my efforts in entirely different areas (in spite of not having any money). I could have invented for them not only the wheel (that's easy) but (more important) the axle and axle grease. But, I'm wondering, How could I have brought them fire so that they wouldn't have burned themselves? But perhaps these are not the real people of this planet at all, but descendants of Neanderthalers or abominable snowmen, here in the primitive outer reaches of society, living on the slopes of mountains or at the edges of the deserts. (No wonder they're hairy.)

Time is still passing right here and now, however, and quite rapidly (as before). The twins' rate of growth is disappointing. (Hosay One and Hosay Two. *He* named them. That doesn't mean I love them any less.) They still don't say Muth-uh very well and sometimes I wonder if they ever will, and they are looking much more like him than like me. But the way the minds here are growing weaker every generation (not to mention the political situation), I suppose they will seem quite normal when they are sixty-five or so. Until that time, I will feign a gay insouciance (all the while awaiting either talent scouts, rescue from the skies, or archetypal man, whichever comes first.)

But quickly, before he says I'm up to my old tricks again, let me ask, Why can't I make as much money as a good whore? "You think this is all just science fiction," I say. "Why, you still believe in the old sawing-a-woman-in-half trick and the disappearing ten of diamonds. What can I say to you?"

I don't tell him, but I'm afraid that rather than continuing my journey through space and time, I will have to continue it only through time, and (usually) there's something to look at out the window everyday. And one isn't much sadder up there in the sky watching galaxies fade by. Why should I worry? Why should I talk so much and so loud? Why should I stay alert to the differences between us, them and me? And then why shouldn't I croak and groan now and then, dizzy, having fallen down?

Secrets of the Native Tongue

I HAD BEEN INVITED to participate in a symposium on modern linguistics, which I know absolutely nothing about, but my transportation would be paid, I would be put up in what was described as a hotel of nineteenth-century grandeur only one block from the beach, all meals would be included as well as the banquet at which I would be expected to give the keynote address. I was wondering why I, of all people, had received this invitation when I noticed that two of the letters of my name were wrong and two other letters were reversed; so I thought: Of course. The invitation is meant for someone else with almost the same last name as mine. However, it did have my correct address, and since my last name is a hard one and is frequently misspelled, I wrote back accepting the invitation.

I have refused so many things over the years, I think it's time to accept something—time to reach out, particularly to the world of knowledge and success. This could be the first step of many steps to come in a general plan for self-enrichment.

And it isn't as if I don't have a few weeks to prepare for it: time to dip into some books on the subject; time to take a few public-speaking classes; time to take (consecutively) one-week cram courses in French, Spanish, and German; time to lose a little weight (possibly all of fifteen pounds by then); time to buy a whole new wardrobe two sizes smaller, get rid of my (I must admit it) slovenly look, wear a lot of eye makeup.

I might not have accepted so quickly if I hadn't, as a matter of fact, already embarked on a massive campaign of self-improvement, at least to the extent that I had already made out long lists of things to do and not do from now on: get up earlier, clean up, eat less, holler less, smile a lot, and so forth. Also become adept at something, if only one little thing. Show what I'm capable of, whatever that may be (thought why not modern linguistics?). Opportunities have been few—have been lacking altogether, actually. My own fault. I've read that. Always your own fault and I suppose that's true. But for one thing, I thought life would be a lot longer than it is. I thought there would be *time*. That things would happen; but now, something *is* happening. I feel pretty good as I mail the acceptance. I think I'm right to say yes, even though I can no longer consider myself to be an object of desire.

Ludicrous to attempt to appear younger. Perhaps, at my age, ludicrous to attempt anything at all, but I keep telling myself that it is no small feat to have gotten this far. It must have taken a modicum of courage merely to stay alive in the face of the many setbacks of a long and neither particularly happy nor productive life. . . . But, actually, I've not had setbacks. To fail, one must have, I suppose, tried. Well, now I will.

Courage! I tell myself, for now even more courage will be called for. There's the fear of academics to be dealt with, and the fear of those who write books, the fear of experts, and of course, the fear of men in general and women, too.

In Saussure I find out that the linguistically significant parts of the vocal apparatus are lips, tongue, upper teeth (I had not realized that the lower teeth are not directly involved with the production of language. That's one of their secrets I've learned already), the palate (front and back), uvula, glottis. . . . "The oral cavity offers a wide range of possibilities." I memorize it to repeat at some later time, should the occasion arise. I'm thinking that while I'm at this symposium I might even create a few new words myself, and perhaps if I try hard, I can discover one new sound in which the lower teeth *are* linguistically significant.

In spite of all my careful preparation and my feeling that I've come, in the last six weeks, closer than I've ever been before to being an intellectual of sorts, the moment I enter the hotel lobby I see that I have made a terrible mistake. I forgot that academics are inclined to rumpled browns and grays, to corduroys and tweed; to, if elegance at all, a simple elegance—even the women. My new clothes are all wrong. (Unfortunately I have dressed to impress myself, not them.) I hunker down into myself as I register at the front table, but they notice me anyway. I sign my name as I always do. I'm not pretending I'm that other name. They look at each other and whisper. "She's here. That's the one." I hear it all down the hall. I don't speak to any of them. I hurry to my room, remove the heavy jewelry and comb my freshly blued gray hair into a knot behind my head. Wipe off all my lipstick but leave the eye shadow and my nice new long lashes. Unfortunately I have only one black sweater with which to cover up my glitter, my peacock greens and purples (and it's hot) and I have no other shoes than these of silver. Perhaps I can transcend my clothes with my dignity. Or perhaps I can be incomprehensible in the best sense of the word. Ambiguous. Enigmatic. At any rate, I will try to stay in the dim light (if there is any) and look proud, but at the same time, sincere—very sincere.

I come back down. Enter grand ballroom for the opening reception. I'm trying to forget that I was already seen by many of them in the lobby with my blue hair piled on top of my head. No dim light. I hear again those: "There she is. Here she comes," and so forth. How to walk in with everyone looking at me? Keep head up. Affect a slight springiness of step, toes first, hands extended just a tiny bit, balance perfectly centered (as best I can, that is, on these high heels), not too much roll from side to side (black sweater buttoned to the neck). . . . Why—a whole room full of them here—and standing upright on two feet as though it were the most natural thing in the world! They've gotten used to it and so have I (balancing) just as if it hadn't taken a million—maybe millions of years to evolve to this point. As if it was perfectly normal to be walking around on their hind legs, to be hairless except for a tuft on the top of the head and tufts here and there in other places, and to be (and completely arbitrarily!) one or the other of two existing sexes. Alive and in a state of uncertainty! Alive and in motion and at this single point in time! I can hardly breathe at the wonder of it.

And here *I* am, upright and among them!

Well, I always did yearn to wake up some day as a completely different person and in a completely different place. I think from the moment I knew that I was I, somehow it wasn't the right "I." Perhaps now it is, and I am changed *enough*. I am who I've always wanted to be. And (and also as I've always wanted) here I am appearing suddenly as the mysterious stranger from who-knows-where? So everything is coming true, and finally. You make your own life, they say, and I'm doing that at last and it's not quite as hard as I thought it would be, because here I am now, already surrounded by several scholars from distant universities. All admiring me. I hope I don't inadvertently let slip a grammatical error.

"I'm glad you finally decided to attend one of our little gatherings. I've appreciated your books so much."

Books! My God, why didn't I think to look up the books I've written instead of struggling through all that Saussure, Fries, and Todorov? I don't even know the titles of them. Still, I find, at least for the moment, that there's not much I'm called upon to do in the way of response except to say "Thank you" and "how nice of you to say so," smile a lot, murmur once or twice phrases I've memorized such as "Explication du texte" and "The sign is always arbitrary."

I must be careful, though. Laugh beginning to get too loud. (Mother always said my laugh was raucous.) Certainly such a laugh would take away all my mystery and glamour—if one of my age may be said to have any of either. Still, I don't feel glamour's completely out of the question, nor is the fact that I might have written some of those books, whatever they are. Can appearances—and by appearances I mean this whole setting with myself here, waving my fringed scarf, one plastic bracelet clacking against the others—can appearances lie to such an extent that I haven't even written one of all those books? Or even one little part of one of them? I think not.

"We must abandon our word-centered thinking about language," I venture to say (quoting from Fries). It must have been the right thing for now several young professors of both sexes are asking me to walk out with them to the beach. It seems there's a linguistic volleyball game going on between the tagmemics people and the Chomskyites, and they're asking me to take part. I decline. I say it's because of my age and my high-heeled shoes. They say, of course, "Bare feet" and "You're not old." I laugh from my highest register to low. A bit too loud, I know, but I've done it worse than that and probably will again sooner or later. They leave for the beach, but three young men stay. (The real reason I didn't go was that I didn't know which side I'm supposed to be on or rooting for.)

"And what are you working on now?"

(I've overheard a few things in the meantime and I already have a good answer to that.)

"I'm beginning a long work on the diphthong."

"Fascinating."

They're hanging on my words. They're wondering what I'm going to say next.

"Some fundamental problems still await solutions."

"How modest of you not to have brought any of your books with you."

I'm thinking: Here I am being noticed by important scholarly men and not even all of them young ones, for here come two older ones to join us.

"If you want to consider phonemes over morphemes, that's quite all right with me," I say, more for the benefit of the older men who have just arrived than for the three young ones. The oldest of them seems almost my age and has thick black eyebrows contrasting with his white hair, and very dark, and I think, suspicious eyes. When he looks at me I wonder, suddenly: What of the sensual pleasures of intellectuals at play, and of linguists in particular?

"Are you speaking ironically?" *He* asks it.

I wink and try to look sly. (Actually I've no idea how I ought to mean it.) "Those that are linguistically naive," I say, "do not understand that sound is merely a substance to be put in use by language." I had been surprised, too, when I read this in Saussure. I had no idea either. I confess that now. "Not so long ago," I say, "I had no idea either."

No one answers. Perhaps I shouldn't have confessed.

Then I remember an apt quote from Fries-the-son: "'Language is used to fill awkward silences,'" I say, "'once social contact,' as in this very case, 'has been made.'"

They all laugh. It was the right thing to say. I see that in their eyes—in *his* eyes.

Things go well. By late afternoon my future has already become a foregone conclusion. I have, and in just a few hours, accepted several invitations to lecture at universities all over the country. I've said a tentative yes to taking a job at a well-known college not far from where I actually live. Only two days a week on campus and that's called three-quarters time. (I never realized how easy academic work was though I did know about the long vacations.) "I'm honored," I say, modestly looking at the floor—my silver shoes. I have been saying that frequently this whole last hour, and in truth, I *am* honored. I am, finally, to be given my due. I begin to enunciate every word clearly (especially after this last offer) . . . every syllable, the way the very best linguists would enunciate them. I don't think I've ever been so happy. What it is, is I'm reaping the rewards of my courage. They could, all of them, do worse than to learn from me.

What I've needed all these years was just a little praise. I didn't understand that until right this very minute, now that I've had the courage to come and get it. There's a TV set in my room here at the hotel and I'm sure there's a good Saturday afternoon movie on, but would I watch it! Not with that older man looking into my eyes. (Though where has he gone?)

By now there's a large crowd in the room. One can hardly push one's way across it, but suddenly I hear a rustling — a whispering. People pull back, pressing against each other, leaving me exposed and alone, and as though I come from another world entirely.

Hold glass by stem, first finger and thumb only. Take one sip. Force laugh back, and instead, smile. Confidently. Across the floor the real me appears. I don't know how I know, but I do. It is *the* Isabella Présempailles.

She's very small and dressed all in brown, several shades of it. She's like them in their tweeds and corduroys. Hair pulled back. Can't weigh more than ninety at the most. Flat-soled shoes, though she could use more height. I would tower over her even without my high heels. Beside her is that man with the black eyes and caterpillar eyebrows. He is whispering into her ear. He has to lean far down to do it. I may be old, still I was hoping for a lover from among the learned — the mysterious learned (though not any longer quite so mysterious since I myself have become one of them). But all this time the look in his eyes was suspicion. That would account for the stary quality. The piercing look that I had hoped was meant to undress me really only wanted to undress me figuratively speaking.

It's so quiet you can hear the sound of the waves outside. No, no. It's the air-conditioning system.

Suddenly she, the real me, begins to sneeze. Probably an allergy. Her nose is red. I, too, have been troubled by the same problem, though, surprisingly, not at all since I got here. Fame has been good for me. It has cured my sneezing.

And now I do let my laugh ring out. I lean my head back and laugh like my mother said I never should. "The oral cavity offers a wide range of possibilities," and that's true. It is a diphthong laugh. If I know anything about diphthongs, and I think, by now, I do, this is one — or, rather, several in a row. I don't know how they count them, if by two's or three's or what. I will research that later and put the answer in my new book.

"And this is Madame Présempailles."

It is *he* who introduces us. He says it once, presenting each to each, one name for both.

She sneezes. I nod, looking down at her from my high-heeled shoes.

Are we not, standing here together, living examples of two linguistic viewpoints, the synchronic versus the diachronic? I, the synchronic and in the here and now. She, belonging to the past and (possibly) the future. But I think it's just as well if I don't mention that out loud.

Her allergies make her look terrible, and, sneezing as she does, how can she expect to give the keynote address?

"Who is this person?" I ask, "I didn't catch the name."

"Isabella Présempailles."

"Is this person expected to speak tomorrow night?"

My meaning is clear to all. No one answers. Of course no one can, not even the real me. Not even the handsome older man beside her.

I'm thinking that what she needs is a little fame and fortune such as I have. That would stop those allergies. Shall I tell her that? Lean down and say it, loud enough so *he* will hear me and see the kindness in me? My largess?

I remember an old saying: "Eating a mouse includes its tail." I do owe her something, I suppose, though it sticks in my throat.

But *I* want to be the one to walk out on the beach tonight, if not with *him*, then with some smaller man, or a balding one, or one with ordinary eyes. I don't care as long as it's with some linguist or other of the opposite sex.

There. She has only to look into my eyes to start her sneezing again. There. Her handkerchief is out. As much, I think, to hide my face from her . . . or maybe for her to hide her own face in. Wiping her nose, her alibi. Perhaps that's the purpose of people's allergies. It's why they have them. Perhaps it was that way for me also – hide behind the sneezes, get lost in my handkerchief, not be seen except as that: sneezing. I have been fat for the same reason . . . maybe the same reason that she is very thin. Both of us wanting to disappear one way or another, I, into my flesh, my face unrecognizable, the features all gone to mush. But that has changed. *I* changed it. I took control of my own life. When opportunity knocked, I answered. And one thing I'm sure of is that I am certainly almost *the* Isabella

Présempailles, except for only a couple of misplaced letters. And I have made something of myself these last few weeks, achieved this much so far, which is a great deal. *Her* joys are, clearly, the lonely ones, and she has those . . . has always had them. My joys are these, which she can't deal with anyway, it seems. I will not let them be taken away after all the hard work I've done to make this happen.

"Eating a mouse includes its tail" indeed, but maybe it means the opposite of what I, at first, thought. Yes, I will see it through.

"Is this person expected to speak?" I say it again, this time standing on her foot, the fringe of my scarf hanging down into her eyes.

She has such a sneezing fit then, that she has to leave. There's no question about it, she has to, but I make it so she must pull hard to get her foot out from under mine. *He* goes with her. I'm not surprised. She shouldn't be left alone in that state.

But later on I *am* the one on the beach with *him*. We found each other after supper—he, in running shorts and sweatshirt, and I, hot though it still is, my black sweater buttoned to the neck. (They say sweating takes off pounds, and I can still afford to lose several more.)

"She's a pitiful creature," he says right away, "I could not persuade her to come out to watch the sunset." He looks at me (piercingly). "You two are so very different."

"'In language there are only differences,'" I say, quoting Saussure again, "and I suppose that's true in life, too."

"A complicated situation."

And I, again from Saussure: "'Language being what it is, we shall find nothing simple in it.'" Then I switch to Sapir: "'It almost goes without saying that two languages, A and B, may have identical sounds but utterly distinct phonetic patterns.'" Of course I'm thinking how our names are, to all intents and purposes, the same.

"Which are you, A or B?"

I clack out my long, long laugh. It's getting so I'm not as afraid of it as I was when Mother was around, but even so, I know Mother was right. It's a nervous laugh and certainly of the lower classes. Not a single one of the linguists has a laugh at all like mine.

"'A mouth and an ear are different organs,'" I say, only slightly misquoting Miller. (How can I go wrong if I stick, basically, to quotes? Certainly I won't inadvertently sound uneducated or perhaps even uncouth.)

Now he's laughing. It was a serious quote which I found in the middle of a scholarly article, but he's laughing.

"That's from George A. Miller," I say.

The sun has gone down. I hardly noticed. It was *him* and his stringy legs I was looking at. Stars are popping out.

"I believe we met a long time ago," he says. "I remember out on the end of a dock. We lay on our stomachs and watched the water lapping around the pilings, and the stars reflected in it. Do you remember any such thing? It was you, I think. You were . . . thinner. . . ."

"You know," I say, "what really did surprise me . . . I mean, I was surprised that I hadn't known it before, and that was that," (and then I quote from Fries) "'The graphic shapes we call *numerals* are not alphabet signs but *word signs*.'"

"I never know how to take you," he says and laughs again. "But I gather you don't want to remember. I suppose it's just as well."

"The simplest thing one can do in the presence of a spoken utterance is to listen." (From Miller again.) But I really do want to remember.

"I wonder that you never married."

That's something I've often wondered myself. Am I so ugly? So repulsive and I don't even know it? And yet why would anyone have lain prone with me on a dock watching waves if I hadn't had some attraction? I wonder, though, would I have sacrificed my linguistic career for marriage? Might I sacrifice it even now? It isn't too late.

"Is it so out of the question," I say, "that I might marry, even now, at my age and at the height of my career?"

"You were a tiny little thing. Wearing a black bathing suit, I think. Your hair, beginning to dry and curl back up."

"You have remembered it all these years."

"That was Wisconsin. In those days you came to the meetings."

"Yes."

Had he kissed me, I wonder, one oral cavity against another? Had he put his arm around me? Had we, even. . . . I would have been attracted to him at first sight, just as I was this afternoon. It had been like it is right now, only we are supine, not prone, and the stars are up, not down in the water as they were then.

"It was like right now," I say.

The waves lap, lap, lapping. How could anyone forget it? The weathered boards of the dock. His arm around. . . . Not now. Then.

"It's an odd name, yours. There's an opera singer by the same name, or rather, almost. She spells it differently. A couple of letters. Have you heard of her?"

That he suspects me of not being a linguist has been clear from the start, but that he suspects me of being an opera star! . . . I only just understood it now. I see, though once I think about it, that it's an easy mistake for him to make, all my faults, those of a prima donna: fat, loud, flamboyant clothes, my laugh (it must span octaves), my silver shoes. . . . He has recognized me as that other. Shall I hum a bit? Quietly so he doesn't hear that I can't carry a tune?

I lie, odalisque, propped on one elbow, looking up at the stars. "You like opera," I say.

"Yes, and I like that singer, too."

He likes her! (Fat as she is.)

His voice is right in my ear, soft and close and male. Especially that. Very little in my life has had to do with anything male. But why haven't I married! Indeed, why didn't I do it a long time ago instead of wondering why not all the time? At twenty I wondered. At twenty-five, twenty-six, thirty-seven, and on and on, wondering, what's wrong with me? But he said, a little thing in a black bathing suit, my wet hair beginning to curl again. Nothing wrong there. I sense an answer, hidden and simple. Still, would I sacrifice a career in *opera* for it? That's even more exciting than being a scholar and a linguist. But he likes her! And just as she is. And there . . . up there in the sky, the whole universe all spread out! Knowledge surrounds me. I feel it tingling in my bones. Answers, hidden and simple. Hidden and simple. Divide the universe into units, smaller and smaller units: on/off, 1/0.

I tell him, "Up there it's exactly as it is in language, there are only contrastive minimum pairs." And then I quote from Fries, "'The important question is always . . . are the two . . . like or different.' Even as you and I are just such a contrastive pair as we sit here now, how odd that the universe should be made up of such as we, and how simple it is once one sees that." (I do not say it, but I'm thinking that of the 1 and the 0, I know which of us is which.)

But he's laughing again. Somehow I've broken the spell that I had hoped to create: the mystery and the whole universe thing that I had wanted in it.

"I never know how to take you," (again) "but I suppose your attitude is all for the best and I appreciate it."

Why, I'm wondering, and, what attitude? But if he should lean close to me and say, "I know your secret," I would say, "I know you know," and then I would hum for sure. I know very little opera, but I think I could fake a rendition of the *Toreador Song* though that hardly seems appropriate. Isn't there a Queen of the Night and a Venusberg? But things are not turning out right at all, and now he's getting up. I wanted magic moments. I wanted his voice in my ear here in the dark like it was. I wanted to *confess*. Have I gotten sand in my hair for nothing? Perhaps ruined my shoes?

"I know your secret."

Now he says it, standing up and looking out to sea. It's clear he's about to go back to the hotel.

"I know," I say. I'm on all fours in the sand, struggling to my feet. At my age (and size) it's not so easy to get up anymore, from so far down. I'm glad he's not watching.

"And I, I married someone else."

"I know," I say, though I didn't until just now. (So that's my reason for never marrying. It makes a lot of sense.)

I'm up, finally, and without any help. He's still looking at the surf. I had been thinking that with the universe out there and all, anything could happen, but it didn't. There's one more day, though, and other men, and the keynote address. I'm eager to end this evening and get to sleep and then to get up and get on with it. "Let's go," I say.

The next morning there's volleyball again. I know who's side I'm on by now. I wonder, is *she* out there playing, jumping around in her long brown skirt and black oxfords and wiping her nose? Not likely. Maybe I should play, then. Show how different we are. Yes, I will. (If she did play, we would be on the same side, of course: for tagmemics, anti-Chomsky.)

And I do play, though not well. *He* plays beside me so I'm trying hard to be graceful. It's him I want to impress, but every time I try for grace—left arm extended behind me, fingers pointing up, right hand delicately poised—the ball goes right by. In fact, through the whole game I never do hit the ball except once, with my head. It bounces off me and down to a little bald man who then scores. It's our only score. Of course the Chomskyites win. Even though I've heard them arguing (and hotly) all weekend, nobody seems to care much. Perhaps they are just being kind since I had had such a role in losing the game. I had set my silver shoes on the sidelines and played barefoot. With shawl, though. I had thought to swing it back and forth as I ran here and there with little steps. And I did that—ran from one end to the other. I was always in the way, and so we lost. Yesterday they had won. I am wondering what all this will mean linguistically, and I am thinking that I must not think about myself so much, and that tonight, especially, I will not think, but do and be exactly what I am regardless of what I look like and whether graceful or not.

I think this as I dress for the banquet. I put my bluish hair back up the way I had it when I first came in. I put on the dress I bought for the occasion, silver and pink and full of pleats. It makes me look fat. I see that only just now, but no more deceptions. The truth, or one loses the game, and I may lose all I have accomplished so far. Nothing but—then—the truth, from now on. What if I had hit the ball once or twice and gotten it over and not cared how I looked? What if I had not run back and forth so much? What if I had paid attention to the game? No, I won't even care that my silver shoes are spoiled by the sand and the wet. I won't care whether I laugh or not. I'll be the real me (whatever that is).

At the banquet I am placed at a long table above the other tables, next to me, the dais. On my other side, *he* is sitting. The Isabella Présempailles, still all in brown, hair-do exactly the same as yesterday, is down there, almost lost, off to the right and at the back. Just the sort of spot she'd choose to be in. I might not have found her at all if I hadn't heard sneezing.

I'm sticking to my resolution to be the real me. I eat and eat—his dessert as well as my own and then another from farther down the table. I laugh octaves of my laugh. It's musical even without my trying to make it so. And then the time comes. He gets up and introduces Isabella Présempailles. How hard I've worked, he says, there by myself, and what a lot I have accomplished, and that now I am working on a book on the diphthong. Only such as I would have thought it needed so much work. Only such as I would have understood the significance. Only I. . . . And, for certain, there will be new and startling conclusions.

(Perhaps I should have been working on that sound I wanted to find that uses the lower teeth in a linguistically significant way. I could have gotten up and made it right now.)

And then I do stand up.

I know what they mean now by "applause in waves," surfs of applause, the grinding of pebbles one against the other and then the rush of ocean, up, towards me. Over me. Mine. What I've always deserved. It is for this moment that I came. I didn't know it when I said I'd come, but it was for this and not even for *him.* Not even for all those job offers, but for this.

I bow and bow. They stand up. They can't stop clapping and I could have wished they never did, but then at last, they do, and there's silence. All eyes on me.

I have had my moment.

And now there are quotes . . . a hundred . . . a thousand quotes ready on the tip of my tongue. One in particular pops into my head (from Firth): "The situations which prompt people to utter speech include every object and happening in the universe." That's true. And true also for song, I'm thinking. Every object and happening in the universe, something to sing about.

I stand here, upright, and large as I am, balanced on two small feet. Actually just on my toes and my spiked heels. It's a miracle . . . a millions-of-years miracle. And, "The oral cavity," as Saussure said, "offers" (offering me!) "a wide range of possibilities." I won't need quotes. I open my mouth. I laugh my laugh, and then I begin to sing . . . about the universe.

The Futility of Fixed Positions

For the sake of clarity, a strong, avian nose. A pose not to be confused with the same pose by any other man. Head, not so much raised, but as though pulled from the shoulder, up, as though about to be lifted, so that, in the whole body, a sense of about to move forward. The eyes are half closed. Waiting, one could think, for a reason to open wider, and yet that reason does not manifest itself. The thoughts—and I do think I know something of the thoughts—preoccupied, certainly, with self, frequently with digestion. It's preoccupation with the stomach that gives that proud and philosophical look. His digestion has always been bad, or at least, he is always noticing it and complaining of it.

What little bit he knows of love, I think I taught him. Not that I have much to give in that line—my skills all lie in entirely other directions—but I knew enough, even in those early days, not to kick the cat.

"Correct me if I'm wrong," he says. I do, I do, and willingly. And he's often wrong. I tell him so and he's grateful for it. In the long run, that is. Recently I struck him (lightly) to rebuke him. He had taken (or so I thought for just a moment) vaguely the outlines of a moose, and with the dignity of a moose, had proceeded with his comments in spite of my whispering into his huge and mooselike ear that he should retreat, and quickly, into the background. I had not, and I admit it, waited for a more suitable moment to reprimand him. I had allowed myself to do it on the spot and in front of two other people, but he behaved like a gentleman, not, at this time, grabbing me by the ankles and pulling me out of my chair.

And I think I can, in general, call him a gentleman. In his own way, that is. Yes, generally a gentleman, with all that that means, especially in terms of aloofness. But kindly and thoughtful, no, though often worried that someone might think him not. But if he is (and it's true, he is) so preoccupied with seeking approval, fame and praise, etc., from the populace, who is there left in all the world to praise *me*? I have often asked him that and will again I'm sure.

"The universe," he says, "has need of abstractions."

Recently, while studying (with the help of a T square and ruler) the connections between music and architecture (and in a moment of deep preoccupation with pillars, plinths, triads, angles, and appoggiaturas), it occurred to him that one must move away, in the end, from seeking universals to seeking the universe. For that thought alone, he has achieved, or so he tells me, recognition of a sort. He says that laying this foundation for some future magnificent piece of work by another man is not an insignificant accomplishment. Others have not done so much in whole lifetimes of effort.

Having achieved this much and proud to have done so, he has already turned to a different kind of study. Now he is hoping to be able to reduce emotions to their essentials and to arrange them in a hierarchy where "love," as he says (quoting Mallarmé), "must be given no more consideration than fear, remorse, boredom, hate or sadness." To Mallarmé's group of emotions he has added several of his own choosing: loathing, malaise, mild psychological distress, deep depression, contempt, pride, jealousy, rage, and blame, among others.

He saves the best emotions for last: ecstasy and joy, fervor, exhilaration, and so on, but he says he has no desire to feel one emotion more than another. He would want to make sure to give them all equal time in his poems if he wrote poems. Also though, as he says, all these emotions are going on consecutively inside him almost all the time, he generally hopes to exhibit a placid exterior. And it's true, he has managed to look placid and completely unconcerned under almost all circumstances as long as I've known him, which is well over forty years.

My own feelings tend more to the simple love/not-love sorts. That is, am *I* loved or am *I* not? My moods swing on that fact alone. Unfortunately I can never read his face. As I said, it is deliberately bland, though perhaps if I dared to look into his eyes . . . . They are small and deep set and, as already mentioned, half-closed; but I know, from some old memories, that they are blue. Not a brilliant blue, but blue enough nonetheless.

He has always maintained that the door must remain shut between us and that we should, except occasionally, remain on our respective sides of it. He says I must make an effort to keep quiet and out of his way. Also an effort to protect him from everyday life that it not impinge on his working time. He believes that sex is an excuse for not doing productive work . . . an alibi. He doesn't want to fool himself with sex. He is always telling me he can't think about other emotions coldly and abstractly when I'm around bothering him. He says he is not concerned with mere irritableness nor with mood swings. He says real emotion is something quite different . . . something quite beyond the depressing fog in which we view each other. He says, "Find someone else to share your little life with or stay with me, as you wish, but I'm telling you you'll regret it when you start cooking and washing socks for someone not worth cooking and washing socks for."

I was going to leave. I've said I would before. Even made it as far as the back seat of the car where I spent a tearful hour examining my own emotions and in their usual order: rage, guilt, hopelessness, then dependency, then love . . . one sort of love or at least it feels like love sometimes. And then what if he *does* become a famous man someday?

But now, suddenly, everything changes and he says wild mood swings count. This morning's brief bout of rage and grief brought a glimmer of interest. I could sense it even before he said anything. "If you must suffer, why not suffer for a good cause?" He only wants the facts. The "what" not the "why."

I never thought that I myself could become the object of his studies. I never even hoped for it. It'll be nice to take part in some real way. Actually, I have already grown fat in order to give myself some reality in his eyes . . . some substance. To be worthy of note, if only as a fellow creature large enough to attract attention now and then. Large enough to be hard to ignore. It was the only alternative. At barely five feet, one doesn't say, stand tall. One doesn't bother to pull one's self up to one's full height. Neither does one say to one's self, Speak up, when one's voice, under stress, turns squeaky.

So I never thought I'd be allowed into the laboratory, or to share in the long, deep thoughts, or sit waiting and watching as he thinks them. But now I'm thinking that perhaps someday I may even have my name alongside his on some article or other, or on a book he may write, as: "Assisted by my wife of forty-eight years, with love (of a sort) and appreciation. Without her, the book would not, could not, exist." Something like that.

Can I do it properly, whatever it is he wants me to do? Will I try too hard? What if a serious failure of emotionality right at the moment it might do me some good? Can I, at the very least, take on the appearance of emotion? And what will the first emotion be, humiliation or ecstacy?

Standing mooselike at the laboratory door (the sweaty smell, the dull eye), he towers above me, thin, with paunch. He is wondering if I'll be willing to submit to some mild forms of torture.

Now if he tells me he never loved me, I'll know it's to elicit an emotional response. If he calls me insane it's for a special reason. Perhaps it always has been. It would be nice to think so.

Enter room. Not much there after all. One big, comfortable chair with footstool. Several small tables piled with papers. No empty space left on any of them to write. Must write in chair. Yes, clipboard there. Paper in it. At the top of page: A MANUAL OF DESPAIR AND ANNOYANCES. Under that: Chronic reality, with a question mark. Then, and underlined: Alternatives to strong emotions, exclamation point. After that, a short paragraph. I read it while he clears papers off a straight chair for me to sit in.

> One evening when all desire and fascination had gone out of my life, I felt, for the first time, what I like to think of as the vertigo common to poets and philosophers, in fact, to artists and scientists of all sorts, though only the best. And in this state I experienced what might be called an emotion beyond all other emotions, and what's more, completely abstract, and with it I felt a satisfaction beyond satisfactions, and yet the world was dull . . . *at last dull*, it seemed to me, and I thought: I am no longer a lover, but this was long ago and now I . . . .

But already he is sitting in the big chair and I'm sitting in the little one as though I acquiesce to everything that may happen here, and evidently it's wired because he has pushed a button and given me a mild electric shock. I managed to hold myself stiff and pretended it hadn't happened. I wouldn't give him the satisfaction.

He checks to see if it's plugged in.

"Is everything ready?"

"Remember little emotions, like little virtues, don't count."

"On the contrary," I say.

Perhaps we will start with my own personal tragedy. (If, for instance, he strokes my hand, I will cry.)

"I'd stroke you if . . . . I'd most likely run my hands over your old body as though you were young and beautiful. I'd kiss. I might, that is. I'd probably run my fingers through your hair. Even murmur things. I could have done all these things forty years or so ago, but I would have felt nothing. You may have thought I didn't know about them, but I did. And I could do all those things—think of it—right now and yet feel nothing. You, on the other hand—you see I know you better than you know yourself—you are a creature of everyday life . . . everyday love."

I'm trying to guess which emotion is involved here. I'm trying to feel something. Nothing comes. I was afraid of that. Should I fake it? And if I fake it, will he know? I smile tentatively, but already it's too late.

"Lack of affect." He writes that down.

I'm thinking that if he has, at any time in the past—or the present, for that matter—had a way with women, *I* certainly haven't seen it.

Another mild electric shock.

"You've missed the pleasures of an open mind."

"On the contrary," I say. I'm thinking that, more than anything, I don't want to be known. That I will not be known—especially by him. That I will change so as not to be known. Change now, or at least, soon. To what, though? And for the worse or for the better?

And what if I really did leave? Now while I'm still able to? Out into the other part of the house? My part of the house (kitchen, bedroom). What adventures lie in that direction? What liberation? What conflict? What excitement? But if I don't submit to this, life will probably pass me by altogether and here, it seems, it may be just beginning. And, anyway, I don't want to wander endlessly in search of a smaller man, one who's more interested in sex and less inclined to confrontations with the cosmos.

"I've changed," I say. Nothing like saying it to make one have to do it. So, though I don't know yet which direction of several to make my changes in, I tell him. I say it twice and hope he's listening though I can't be sure if he is or not. Which leaves me pretty much where I was before I said it.

"Lean back, relax," he says, "and shut your eyes." (I don't.) "Now tell me, are you giddy when looking up at the stars? Does the Milky Way scare you out of your wits? Does the thought of aeons make your heart beat faster? And then does that selfsame heartbeat take your breath away? If so, perhaps you aren't as accustomed to the cosmos as I am. Winter/summer/winter/summer/winter again. I suppose you think they're miracles."

"No, no," I say, and, "Yes I do. I *know*!"

"Perhaps you want to rest back into love . . . lean back in it; let the stars turn as they may and take reality in simple, sexual doses (as though that could save you)? And yet, always a little doubt to set at rest no matter if in love or not."

But I am staring at the far wall on which there is a monochromatic picture of a famous bridge. It is nothing but shadows (as is this room). I forget the name of it though I know I should know it . . . did know it once. So much for the names of things. I'm remembering that he once told me if only he could have a street named after him, no matter how small—one small street, one alley, one court, is all he asks—he'd feel much better about mortality, but I say it's not enough. I have frequently forgotten whole cities, so that even if a hundred alleyways were named after him it couldn't help much.

" . . . no joy other than in this" he says. (I didn't catch the first part. It may have been important.) "So instead of a return to bourgeois values, always a little doubt to set at rest."

Was that a question or is an emotion called for? I pick the first emotion that comes to mind and squeeze out a tear. Only one. One would think an isolated tear would be too small a thing for him either to notice or, if noticed, to admit the existence of, but now he is leaning forward and touching my knee. It's been a long time since he did that. (He has always preferred being close from a distance and often said so.)

"I could laugh *with* instead of *at*," he says. "We could see eye to eye if only for an afternoon."

I can feel the tear drip down my cheek to chin and fall on my collar bone. Stops there. Not enough substance to it for it to go any farther.

"I could look at you with delight. You'd see it on my face. I have devices right here in the laboratory. Devices you've never heard of. Something to drink. Something to smoke. I could promise an experience you've never had before with anyone, least of all with me. Afterwards, inner peace for sure. I could promise that or something very near it."

"If that's a question, the answer is yes."

And there *is*, I see it now, a strange contraption collapsed in the corner of the room, partly hidden behind a pile of old newspapers, a rocking device with harness and with what might be wings. Combination black leather and black lace (some pink) and a bicycle seat, the long narrow kind for men. Has this been my rival all these years? However, cobwebs on it now and a lot of dust. Looks flimsy. Might be broken already by the look of it. How back out gracefully if offered a ride on it, I wonder? (He hasn't kept himself as pure as I thought.)

But now — his finger must have slipped or (and I do know it's true) tears make him angry, though this was only one — but now, a severe electric shock. I come to, head hooked on back of chair, my legs stiff out in front of me. As I try to sit up, I fall flat on my back on the floor. I turn from supine to prone, telling myself I should — could if I wanted to — at least be sympathetic. After all, he's probably having a hard time too. All this work and still no fame at all that I can see. All the days cooped up in here. And who, if not I, to understand him? Who, if not I, to stay with him, loyal to the end? The very end. Who, if not I, no matter what happens? Still, all the failures do reflect on me. And perhaps a man gets the kind of love (as they say is the case with governments) the kind of love he deserves. Am I it, then? Do I serve some higher purpose not of my own choosing, merely a sort of sidelight of his life? The avenging angel or some such thing?

I turn and bite him on the ankle. Rather hard, I think. (Should I have kissed it instead, avenger or not?) But it's partly to attract attention — to say, Here I am down here, you blockhead. As though the world were not already painful enough as it is, he kicks out in annoyance. I think he thinks it's the cat. He's haunted me before just like this in my nightmares, kicking out at me in almost this same way, and though I might think I don't deserve it, it isn't as if I've lived my life without complaining, or had many moods of cheerful affection.

But I think I *have* changed. I don't think I would done such a thing as bite a few minutes ago . . . or, at least, not done it quite like that, through the sock and all (and not a very clean one, either). I believe I am quite different and becoming more so all the time. Certainly my next move is as unknown to me as it must be to him. I am, at last, unfathomable. Perhaps not to be grasped in a whole year of close observation. Just what I've always wanted to be: a surprise, whether a pleasant one or not. Also I can suddenly remember the name of that bridge, but have, for the moment anyway, forgotten *his* name (not to mention my own).

"The cosmos," he is saying, "is not as simple an object as some people seem to think, nor on the other hand, as complicated as might be supposed by those who needlessly complicate things."

Suppose I could short-circuit not only the chair, but this whole area of the house? I look around on the floor for something metal. See a piece of yellow paper with a list of facts to face, FACTS TO FACE written along the top. Under that such things as bleeding from the mouth; the death of children, especially one's own (we have no children); being left out in the rain or—worse yet—sleet, and at night, no stars, just a reddish glow; being caught in a trap for a large animal or buried alive; bitten by a rabid rat (also at night, same red glow), or the dream of it and waking up screaming; and so on and on . . . . *I* have already faced every single one of these facts, and a long time ago, and would tell him so to his face if I didn't feel all tingly and happy-as-I-am for once, ears still ringing.

"And," he says, "speaking of the cosmos, a glimpse of it can sometimes make a man either less or more forlorn, depending on if the man has status or not. I suppose it's the same with woman."

I don't say, "on the contrary," because now I don't want him to notice me down here on the floor, but I'm thinking it's the hand on the knee or the lack of, and not only not on the knee, but not on other places either, or seldom . . . though perhaps one is really forlorn because one's breasts are no longer as firm as they used to be.

He says, "If only my name had been Anatole or Marcello or (and especially) Nicanor! . . ."

Well, that's several names to cross off the list if I went to bother finding out what name he goes by, but not worth the trouble. What about, on the other hand, the unlived (so far) part of my life? How to pass it? She smiles, she cries, she pleads, she rages, she makes up. Nothing new in any of that.

I stand up and stretch. He's still talking.

". . . If, on the other hand, my name had been Roland or Tristram or Ezra or Somerset, love would have been an entirely different thing for me, and poetry also."

But I'm at the door already and I leave, closing it with a bang. He calls out after me, "I knew you'd go."

I turn around and come right back.

"I knew you'd be back," he says.

I go to the corner and pick up the contraption collapsed there. Though awkward, it's not heavy. Then I really do leave, closing the door gently this time.

"I knew you'd leave," he shouts, "but you'll be back."

Paralysed for a moment by the image in the hall mirror of my wrinkled face with its halo of wispy white hair, overwhelmed for a moment by something resembling the truth: What if the cat, for instance, represents one form of the universe as we — as he — knows it? Or myself, for that matter, and other things playing roles I cannot even guess at? But once outside the front door, all my tears are for myself. Stars out. No clouds. Brisk breeze. Moments like this in my life have been few and far between. Courage, I tell myself. (If anyone asks me what I'm doing out here at this time of night, I'll say that I'm renaming all the streets for Nicanor.)

He said I'd be back. Well, maybe so; but does one return to a house one has forgotten the address of as well as the name of the principal occupant? Does one return when one has the (possible) source of one's own pleasures hanging over one's shoulder, so to speak, or, as he said, a chance at inner peace or something very near it?

I place the contraption on the dewy grass of the front yard, get on it and start pumping as hard as I can. I'm not thinking moose, moose, but Nicanor . . . Nicanor . . . .

What Every Woman Knows

We all remember when we first became vaguely aware of them and their sex organs and began to think about them. Later there were those long, long talks about them during which we rated each of them on a scale of one to one hundred; classified them, grouped them, compared them with each other; measured their breasts, waists, hips with our eyes and our fingertips just as we have measured our own penises against those of our fellows. Sometimes, giggling, we entertained each other with a song and dance not unlike what they might do. Still later we began to write words and music about them (their looks and our exploits in relation to them).

There are many things that we enjoy about them, not the least of which is that the smallest of us can generally find one among them even smaller. Still, we have mixed feelings about them, and sometimes hurt pride, though that never shows in our talk.

We've protested against them and we've made laws and a great many rules but they have broken them, sometimes when we least expected it.

Until lately we've kept them out of our domains, preferring that they should live in hinterlands and side streets, outlying districts where we've tried to make them as comfortable as possible according to their own special nature. We left them to their own devices there, hoping they would leave us to ours.

We crossed the river daily.

When we brought them with us we pointed out the sights.

Until lately we protected them.

Until lately we have loved some of them, those with the best figures and features and especially those with long, blond hair.

Until lately we have lived quite harmoniously with them.

We have kept from laughing.

We have tried to be serious about their sex organs.

But now that we have already probed space and sent our engines to the ocean floor, now that we have climbed all the highest mountains worth climbing, and having cracked the atom and the DNA code, we are at the last frontier. Needless to say, we will be discreet. We will blend into the background as much as possible, and rather than be caught looking at their bodies, we are setting up blinds on the edges of town and are keeping our eyes open for chinks in the walls.

Our knowledge is spotty. We have only ourselves to judge by; still, we can sometimes make well-informed guesses. Much is clearly empirical. We know, for instance, that the right breast is the larger by two to three cc's. We know the nipples rise. We know the vulva vibrates of its own accord after the fashion of electric currents passing through mechanical equipment. Sometimes it makes a weird, wet sound like the sound of a kiss. We know it has teeth, but that they are not visible to the naive eye. In virgins the teeth are small and white and soon fall out, after which the larger, yellow teeth grow. We now have available to us a special, protective sheath which may be bent or gouged, perhaps, but never cut in two.

We know there are seven fully documented cases of the female rape of males.

Once upon a time the women lived in small, food-gathering groups. They slept wrapped in their hair, huddled against their brothers and sisters, babies at their breasts, and they planned their days one at a time. There was no other way. It was in that period that we worshipped *them* and took *their* bodies as the norm. We took their names and they took our fatherhood and thanked us for it, taking appropriate action to ensure conception. Even then they had not only secret ceremonials and drugs that could make you feel like flying, but secret implements of implantation and secret ways to satisfy their needs. For four days of every moon they slept in menstrual huts or soured milk at home. The cheese spoiled. The butter wouldn't churn. Their sexual desires waxed and waned according to their cycles while we, not knowing any better, left at their most desirous times and were out hunting bears or lions or off on ships, depending on our geographical location. Later they developed that very modern organ, the clitoris, and could satisfy each other in an entirely different way.

Does a cat have a clitoris? And if so, why? Horses? Cows? Lizards? Birds? Where is the dividing line between those who have and those who don't? (Fish don't.) And what of the clitellum and the cloaca? What pleasurable feelings are associated with them? And if ontogeny recapitulates phylogeny, and if there *are* pleasurable cloacal feelings, then is that a final proof of the vaginal orgasm?

But we believe woman can be *explained*. Attitudes, for instance, and motivations. Allowed caresses. Sights and sounds inimicable to. Newly discovered erogenous zones (those found in the last year or so). (Remember their main purpose in life may be yourselves . . . as individuals or in small groups of three or four.) What, then, is their basic method of procedure? Note the carefully plotted floor plans of efficiency kitchens where the steps are counted from sink to dishwasher, from refrigerator to stove . . .

A WARNING

Though a woman's body can be considered a useful instrument to be played upon (a) by biological forces in the service of the race in general and (b) by the male human animal in particular; this seldom permits any latitude for creative expression on the part of either partner. And what if the particular woman in question should happen to be a person of wide social experience with an academic background and opinions and convictions of her own (as many of them are)? In that case she should be treated accordingly and we ourselves should be the first to grant it. To a cultured person, then, a woman is neither static (stalled) nor quiescent, but an impulsively moving target, animated by concepts and circumstances beyond our wildest hopes and fears. Hardly anything is to be considered impossible.

But

> "Many women otherwise normal and mature are
> seized with a painful longing . . ."
>
> —Helene Deutsch

We believe that they have tricked themselves. They are outliving their usefulnesses. Though they continually deny it, they have lost the sense of the proper time and place. Nowadays, even on their special days of the month, they try to act like the rest of us, as though nothing were happening to them. They have lost their names and blame others for it and because of it they cannot tell who their real sisters are nor what land they came from.

God is a man.

So are lions and foxes, zebras, tigers, sharks, all dogs and all wolves . . . male. On the other hand, cows, cats, pigeons are "female." Whales, chickens (birds of all kinds except the stork), ground hogs, mice, deer, little monkeys—all female, and also (and declaring them incompetent) otters, beavers, spiders, ocelots and manatees.

This is how it should be.

The sun is male. Let it shine on the vulva for a full eight hours sometime during the summer solstice and a woman will conceive the sun's child. It will be a boy of incredible blondness and beauty. If the woman is black, the boy will have red hair and also be of (in this case a dark) incredible beauty.

Such children exist.

I have seen them on the streets.

I was once such a boy myself. I had the power to turn heads in my direction. It was my mother made me what I used to be before my hair turned dark and I was left with not one single living relative of the opposite sex.

Being the sons of virgins we have problems all our own. We cannot father children. Our mothers fear us, not only like other mothers do, for our size and strength, but for our mystery. But just as—having fed the child—the mother forgets to eat; just as—having taken the child for music lessons over a period of years—the mother feels that she, too, can play the instrument, so the mothers come alive when the sons step to the stage and *our* mothers even more so. In many ways they are no different from other mothers as they creep into their son's rooms listening for the sounds of breathing, or leaning close enough to feel the warmth and leaving reassured, except that our mothers can only tell the difference between the sun and son by one single letter and they remain confused about this difference all their lives.

Our mothers (they say, "My son, my sun.") living one half of a life in which we are the rest (which causes rages and obsessions, strange exacerbations of the psyche, twitches, tics . . .); while we, precocious, hold up in each hand poisonous snakes we strangled before we could walk. She snaps a picture. After that, cries out. Makes me wonder, What is the nature of female satisfaction? Now that she is gone I wonder even more. To me it is a question as convoluted as the meaning of meaning.

DESCRIPTIVE ANALYSIS OF ONE INDIVIDUAL

Appropriately younger. Appropriately smaller. Many skills, some not yet catalogued. Owns nothing. Seen from a distance, awkward and lumpy. Breasts jiggle. Nose, wide and a little strange. Eyes, gray-green, a not unusual color.

I was taking time out to discover more about her. I only wanted *useful* information. Long before I was really ready I met her. Brachycephalic, we leaned our heads together. I was strong and silent. I was saving the best of myself for last. At a convenient time and place I kissed her, felt her breasts and learned valuable information I hadn't found out at the movies. I liked what I felt.

I doubled my precautions when I was around her, letting knowledge of myself seep through to her slowly. I grew a wide blond beard. Frequently I made gestures suggesting passion. I kept looking up at the sky or into her eyes and smiling. I stood with my back to the sun.

But though, and especially at that time, I felt the female had great things in store for me, I waited, wanting to become familiar with her underwear before confronting the situation directly.

In the department of comparative anatomy I compared the anatomies of fifty typical women. I was attentive to details that might have been overlooked by others of my kind. I now know what I like.

In a department of lingerie I attacked the other problem, gaining insights into many strange, pandurate contraptions. I studied all the graceless, lacy trappings and accouterments that give the aura of grace, attentive to details. I know what I like.

Love? I don't want to get into any bungling sentimentality. I will use the word at the proper time.

She says; "Just as you've suspected, I have deep within me many fierce and terrible desires common to all women and that lie waiting awakening by men." She quotes: "Woman were formed from a *crooked* rib." She quotes: "There is no wrath above the wrath of a woman." She quotes: "There are three things that are never satisfied, yea, a fourth thing which says not, It is enough; that is, the mouth of the womb." She quotes: "Let us consider also her gait, posture, and habit, in which is vanity of vanities." She quotes: "If we inquire, we find that nearly all the kingdoms of the world have been overthrown by women."

She quotes:

> "Woman is the Chimacra, . . . its face was that of a radiant lion, it had the filthy belly of a goat, and it was armed with the virulent tail of a viper . . . meaning that a woman is beautiful to look upon, contaminating to the touch, and deadly to keep."*

She says: "Once all women were witches. Several people wrote about it, all of them men."

She quotes:

> "And what, then is to be thought of those witches who in this way sometimes collect male organs in great numbers, as many as twenty or thirty members together, and put them in a bird's nest, or shut them up in a box where they move themselves like living members, and eat oats and corn, as has been seen by many and is a matter of common report?"*

It was by accident I came upon the knowledge of it. Her. Suddenly I felt dizzy. I was looking at her but I could make no sense of anything. Words were only separate words . . . goats and horns . . . living members . . . been seen and is oft report . . . I hadn't planned to act so fast, but what else could I do? I didn't want to seem disinterested, but I knew that I had missed many fascinating and perhaps crucial remarks. Action was called for. There was no recourse but to learn by doing and find out what would happen after that. And, since I wanted to take advantage of her anyway (without seeming to), it may have been the best possible move.

I went from "What are you?" to "Whatever you are," and "Show me one more thing," and she did.

If I had three wishes they would be for the same thing three more times.

She tells me that the Navajos say that the sun is only a shield for another being EVEN MORE BRIGHT! and I believe it. I believe it.

"I have a surprise for you: a penis wider than it's long. Only the heads of the largest states have them like that. Ambassadors, sometimes."

(I keep it up with a bit of fishing line.)

She says my penis is not out of the ordinary but the string, just then, pulls taut and I forget the universe (and its intentions). (Blessings on them after all, breasts removed or not.)

So begins a shift of emphasis, and though, by now, I have a wealth of information into the primordial mysteries of the feminine. (She has told me it was women that were the ones who learned the process of fermentation; they, the guardians of potions and poisons, though how does she know? Women, she says, the snake at the saucer of milk by the door; grandmother spider . . . Fornicaria, goddess of the oven . . . I have a wealth of information already, but I'm afraid that in a little while, I will have lost the notion of end results and reasons.

At first I read the veins on her breasts and make conjectures, but the structure is INSANE! Basic ironies abound. Ambivalences. Whoever cooked this up makes me laugh. (Lightning, for instance, strikes the best people. Jesus, born in a manger like any other corn god.) I laugh even when we are using sex for exercise or to cure a cold.

I found out that "Many female mysteries were taken over by the men, and that in some the men still wore the more primordial woman's dress." (How do they know, especially since there were no trousers?)

I found out that "The men rebelled under the leadership of the sun, slaying all the grown women and only permitting ignorant and uninitiated little girls to survive."

I found out that, "Smitten in the core of her being, the woman rages over the silent mountain heights, everywhere seeks the one who also loves best to walk in the heights . . . ."

In a world full of symbols I draw the sun at my crotch, the moon at my belly button, wanting to make all this into one giant work of art with introduction and explanation for it. Sex will be the best joke in it, starting with the Venus of Willendorf . . . .

*Quotations from *The Great Mother,* an analysis of the archetype by Erich Neumann; and *Malleus Maleficarum* (circa 1490), translated by Rev. Montague Summers.

Not Burning

No, I DON'T BURN BOOKS, I just let them drop away. Fall out of sight. I lose them right on the shelves. Here among the file cards, I still have some power. The power to list or not to list, and to be left out of the lists is to be left out of the library. A book will be forgotten whether I inadvertently forget it or whether I choose to forget it, and that's that.

But, good or even bad, most books used to please me. They pleased me by their heft and by their covers and by the fact that words are used to form them. I liked books as books, pure and simple. I took books before bed instead of aspirin. I took books when I felt a cold coming on. But (and through no fault of my own) my joy in them has become empty. Today I dropped four file cards into the trash. God knows what I have rejected just now . . . lost forever . . . unlisted. They could have been my favorites for all I know. All the better, then, if my old favorites.

There are no clear-cut reasons for the absence of these particular books from the files. (I am not a moralist.) I lose books at random. (Well, not exactly at random since they, all four, came in a row from the same file box. Vogel to Vogelstein. Two Vogels, one Vogelgesang, and one Vogelstein.)

Yes, but you're thinking, shouldn't I, rather, find solace among all these books? Turn to them in times of need? Many of the books in the library are filled with do-it-yourself advice and practical philosophies for every occasion. This day and age there is a book for every problem, and the promise of future happiness at whatever age (though there must be limits). Except it was a book that told me it was time for self-examination. It was a book that said to step back with a cold clear eye, and I did. I looked in the mirror and woke up and saw that I had already grown old. Just like that—old—and sooner than I had expected. (Am I the last to know it?) So now, and because of a book, I am in an unpleasant state of mind, though one would hope, only slightly deranged.

And to think that I have not ever dared all these years . . . not even once in all my whole life so far, to wear a black cape and a broad-brimmed black hat with a red tassel. Fearing the loss of self, I suppose. (Who is it, then, who wants to wear that costume? Become conspicuous? Who would I have been if I had dared to do it? And if I *do* dare to do it, who will I become?)

You will be thinking, I've simply not got hold of the right books. Perhaps that's true. And suddenly it occurs to me that if such books exist, they are probably (of course!) among the very ones I have just thrown into the trash.

I retrieve the four file cards. Find: *Symbols of Decay in Western Civilization*, *Behind the Face Lift*, *The Reality of Fantasy*, and *Capturing Desire*. I will check out all these books and examine them at home. Meanwhile, I will throw four other cards, sight unseen, into the trash instead of these. This time all the authors (and deliberately so) by the name of Young. It doesn't occur to me until I'm on the way home that it's one of these *other* four books that most likely contains the help I need. I rush back up the steps and, breathless, feel my heart skip beats, but the trash has already been taken out. Think: there goes my future, such as is left of it. Still, I do have *Symbols of Decay* . . . . Possibly I can take the decay of western civilization as a metaphor for myself and learn something from it. And *Face Lift*. I hadn't thought of that. Old crone with lifted face (lifted eyelids, lifted neck, lifted elbows?) and still all those backaches, weak knees, hairs on my chin? Perhaps better to (and finally) put on a wide-brimmed black hat and a big black cape. (I'll be found out soon enough, I suppose. Probably a role I can't handle. Probably my eyes will look out from under with an incongruous expression.)

I open, first, *Capturing Desire*. The cover is red, pink, and white and has a sort of wing-like design.

> If I were writing about fishes or birds instead of about desire, then the title of this book would be the *The Capture of Birds and/or Fishes* and then we could go straight to the topic at hand with no preliminaries because we all know exactly what a bird or a fish is, but on the other hand, do we know desire? Even know our own desires? Are we not, in the very midst of our yearnings, obsessed also with their opposites? Can we not say

> that we actually do not want what we think we want, and that we do not want it in exactly the same proportion as we want it, so that we continuously balance between two or three or four loves and their corresponding hates. In other words, we do not try to capture anything at all, neither a bird nor a fish. It is we ourselves who are captured, so that when we reach out to grasp the fleeting moment, it has not yet appeared.

And farther on I read:

> And what of the desire to wear certain strange costumes? That is the desire to be noticed by the beloved in a certain particular and very special way. And what of the desire to stand out in a crowd of beloveds, that they should not turn into hostile strangers. And what of the desire to give someone else their heart's desire? That is simply the desire to be noticed by that person, that that person should become the beloved.

The book jacket shows the author, Marshal Vogelgesang, to be a rather fat, bearded man with squinting eyes. (One wonders is he laughing quietly to himself and at what?) Can't tell if he's tall or short. The dust jacket says he lives right here in the city. The book is old. Add twenty years to the picture and he might be almost my age. I do add twenty years and wonder what he thinks about desires at our time of life?

But now I'm wondering, what if today were the last day of my life — which I don't think it is — but would I, even so, dare to wear that black hat and cape? Wouldn't I rather die, then, with my ingratiating smile? Die as a "Nice Person"? Nice to the very end and perhaps, finally, gain acceptance of whomever happens to be present at the time? Probably some nurse or other. "She was nice," the nurse will say. "She never bothered anybody. She was nice to the very end, though in great pain."

In actuality, I know that I am not at all as nice as I try to seem. Nor am I as helpless as one might think. I can do harm. I want to stress that. Can do great harm and may already have done it and might do it again. And tomorrow, I suspect, more books lost, right behind the head librarian's back.

Saturday I will go — yes, I will — actually go out to look for the cape and the hat and appropriate boots, whatever the cost. But how try these things on in front of the clerks, transforming myself from moment to moment? One minute my drab and mousy self, and the next, an elegant and brooding stranger (at last—at least I hope so). They will be saying: "What is that old lady doing in that hat? Does she think she's twenty, tall and thin and dark?" After I have all the proper things on, then it may be different. And what if I, dressed like that, found my old self dressed like this advancing down the same street but on the other side and in the opposite direction? I would flaunt myself to myself. I would cross the street just to swing my cape around in my old self's face and turn my back on her, the "librarian"! While she is busy with her little file cards, I, older and wiser—though with a wisdom not learned in books—will roam the streets and spend her money.

I read:

> There is an element of surprise in all desire, and an element of mystery. Also an important element of danger . . . of the different . . . (which is why we so often fall prey to infidelities). New fires are lit. A fan of possibilities opens out before one. One hesitates. One says to one's self: "At my time of life?" or, "With my looks and disabilities? My stuttering? my limp?" . . . .

This is just what I was hoping to hear. Yes, I *can* awaken desire in others if I dare the costume, dare to throw the cape back over my shoulder. I will be, if not a treasure, then, certainly, a surprise.

> One doesn't lie loose all day Sunday waiting for desire. One has a plan of action. First, it might be well to cultivate an old desire. Start with what's at hand and then progress to higher and more complicated forms until one reaches the most profound desires of all, the most expansive, the most grandiose . . . .

Yes, I will "start with what's at hand," which is this book, though I really don't feel that going after the man that wrote it will be starting small. In fact, right now, it's the highest I can think of doing. But, starting this high, probably I will progress all the faster to the upper levels of desire, and who can tell where I'll get to and what other heights I'll reach.

I decide to send for the new outfit by mail so as not to put myself through any unpleasantness with clerks and also not to be influenced by their opinions. I know the clerks will say that for my coloring, light blue is better. I do know that's true, and I'm deliberately going against it. I don't want to be distracted from my purpose and needlessly buy a whole light-blue wardrobe that I'll never wear, but I don't trust myself to be able to stick to my black outfit, especially not when faced with clerks eyeing each other behind my back and smiling smiles I don't know quite what to make of.

When the outfit comes, it's even better than I expected; the cloak, soft and thick; the hat, glossy and very Spanish. The high-heeled boots almost fit. I know they will rub my feet, but I can stand that. The hat comes a little too far down over my eyes, but all the better to hide any incongruous expressions I may have.

I read:

> Of course one cannot long talk of desires without talking of sexual desires. Just as one cannot long court disaster without bringing about disasters, one courts desire and up comes sex, because, are not desire and sex made of the same cloth, both originating in the mother . . . in the longing for the breast itself?

So I call up Marshal Vogelgesang. He's actually at home and answers the phone himself. His voice sounds old and tired and, possibly, a little drunk. I tell him I'm from a magazine and want to see him about doing an article on him. He not only believes me, he's pleased and flattered and makes an appointment to see me.

When the day comes, I dress in the outfit and put on more makeup than I generally wear, especially eye makeup. I resist the urge to pencil in a little "hairline" mustache. I like this new self. It's not exactly as good as I had thought it would be, but much better than before. I sidle out into the street trying to remain as unobtrusive as possible. I spurt from doorway to doorway, dash down into the subway and try to lose myself against the wall behind a trash can, but there's no hiding. People stare at me even when I'm in the corner hardly moving. Even on the train, they don't read the ads, they look at me.

So, all eyes on me, I stumble up the subway stairs. All eyes on me, I limp, I shuffle down the sidewalk in my too-big boots, my too-high heels. But I'm making progress towards the fulfillment of my desire.

I will try to assume the gestures of self-confidence. I hum to myself. I practice throwing my cloak back with a flourish. I proceed with wide, teetery steps. I try to force my eyes and eyebrows into an expression of daring . . . even cruelty. I stick out my elbows.

I look sideways at myself in store windows as I go by (though I hope no one sees me do that) and I get a general sense of black on black, of a great swirl of cloak, and a puffy, pale slice of frightened face, full of what could less be called desire and more be called yearning. And yet, if yesterday's self could only see me now! How I'd strut away from her. The thought, I see in the store windows, makes me strut in actuality. I finally have the proper expression. Keep thinking of that old, other self — I tell myself — then everything will fall into place.

I'm thinking that perhaps Marshal Vogelgesang and I will romp through the park joking with each other, even though up to now, I've never been very good at joking. We'll be teasing and flirting and holding hands. I feel so happy at the thought that if I should see my old self walking backwards against the wind at this very moment, I'd let myself be blown clear around the corner. I wouldn't stop to help. I'd laugh. That old thing, I'd think. Let her be blown straight into the East River for all I care. This one here is certainly the better self. Look how I, screwing up my courage, am actually knocking at his door as in *Capturing the birds and fishes of desire.*

Seeing him, I wish I had worn my gray hair down.

He is probably just slightly shorter than I am, though now, in these heels of mine, I tower over him. A pale man with a crooked nose. Not so much fat as soft. Might be a little younger than I am or either better preserved. It's hard to tell. I'm held spellbound for a moment by the way he combs several strands of pale hair across his bald spot. At least that's the only explanation I have for what happens next. "I read your book," I blurt out, "and I have come to give you your heart's desire."

(One faux pas as bad as this one should count, at the very least, as three, and I know I'll get even with myself for this bit of ridiculousness later.)

But now feel the heady pleasure of making an impact of *whatever* sort.

He stands silent. Not answering. Not moving. Who could move? Who could answer? I feel a surge of power. Why, he's just a little man who writes the books, while I can lose them or save them as I see fit, and I have saved *his* book from oblivion. If I had let that card stay in the trash, he might as well not have bothered writing it at all.

I push past him into the room. I stride about, waving my arms. I tip my hat even farther over one eye than it already is. I grin and clench my teeth. "Suh . . . suh . . . suh . . . supposing," I say, ". . . puh . . . puh . . . presupposing that we get to know each other better, of course. Uh . . . uh . . . after the interview, I mean," and I pull out my notebook and pretend to read off carefully prepared questions (though I had forgotten to prepare any):

"When did you first become aware of the contradictory nature of desire—changed, as it always is, by little nudges in the opposite direction?

"Would you say that desire was an art, and that one must have an aptitude for it . . . a special talent? Are there geniuses of desire?

"And if desire *is* an art, what happens to it if and when it comes to pass that, as they say, reality outstrips art? Though, personally, I wonder why either should care? Why pit a bird against a fish, in other words? And can birds be said to be outstripped by fishes? And if a fish does outstrip a bird, or vice versa, what then?

"But what I really want to know is, Have you ever been adored *unconditionally*? Unconditionally adored? I believe, though I'm not absolutely sure of it yet, that I have come prepared to adore, though I know that may be hard to keep up for a long time. So, teach me all about desire. I read your book, but I didn't quite finish it."

(I think I'm doing pretty well considering the fact that I'm making all these up as I go along.)

"If you don't leave instantly," he says, "I'll call the police," but I don't think he really means that.

"I submit," I say, "that you yourself do not know, at this very moment, what you desire. Don't hurry off into your future this way. Take some time. You yourself have written it. Also you said, 'Grasp at whatever joys come your way,' and, 'Life is full of too much questioning and not enough desire.'"

"I don't need this," he says.

"But I think I can give you a short description of my troubled self in only seventeen minutes," I say. "I am an average woman, though I'll let you be the judge of that. Purposeful at this moment, yes, but average in spite of my hat and all these black things, though isn't there a secret desire in everyone to dress in some dashing way so as not to find ourselves dismissed at a glance . . . so as to confirm the fact of our being here, in the world and human, after all, which I am, and full of the terror of it. So, just because I've dressed like this doesn't make me any different from anybody else, though I suppose you don't believe that, but it's true, and when I leave here, if I should see in front of me someone walking along in a print dress (such as I always used to wear) and an old brown sweater that sags at the pockets, I will feel no fear of her, for I have gone beyond myself already today . . . gone beyond myself by coming here, and regardless of what may happen or even what doesn't happen. I thought you would be pleased to know it and would see that I am not unlike your other loves, for certainly you had other loves; I'm aware of that and I accept it. I'm optimistic, you can see, and though I may seem like a trivial being to you, never having written anything though I could have if I wanted to and even started: 'Call me Helen,' I wrote, 'or, call me Edith or Virginia or Margaret . . . .' And thought to end with: 'I was the last,' or, 'next to last.'"

But somehow, in all this talk, a call has been made and police come to take me away.

I don't want to deteriorate into a mass of quivering jelly for other people to stick pins into, so I assume a bold expression. "I admire a man who adheres to his morals," I tell Marshal. "Who stands by *himself*, in other words. I admire that strength of character I find in you. I, too, try for that, and always have . . . ." But by now I'm out of earshot—his ear, that is—and wondering if there isn't some more efficient way for me to go about capturing desire.

It's a good policy, when arrested, to keep quiet and calm and not talk too much. Besides, I'm already all talked out. Besides, I have nothing to say to these men except: "Is there any rule that says I can't wear this kind of a hat?"

Of course they let me go. Just tell me not to do it again. (I don't say yes *or* no to that.) They think I'm harmless and helpless and I let then think so. They even offer me coffee and I take it though I can't drink coffee. It keeps me up all night, gives me uneven heartbeats and indigestion. Always does. But I don't dare refuse.

It's pretty late when I walk out of there and there's an almost full moon coming up behind the buildings. It gives me a big thrill to see it, and I remember something else Marshal wrote:

> One ought to be less concerned with unavailable desires than one is with the inability to desire at all, which is an all-too-common difficulty, and comes about because one is aware of the inexcusable desires one is so full of, and one tries to put them out of one's mind. What if, one wonders, what if there were a climax to all those inexcusable desires at one and the same time! One is in great danger of it and one knows it. An inner uneasiness prevails, and one would rather live with this uneasiness than face the perils of a luminous and vibrant delight.

I think I'm feeling that last right now, though it may be just the coffee.

As I walk to the bus stop, there *is* this lady in sweater and print dress, comfortable shoes, *my* old shoes. I envy her those shoes, but I don't like her chubby, squat shape. I don't like the way she looks around, keeping track of everybody as if she's scared of being mugged. I stride by and laugh as I pass, hoping she hears me and knows it's her I'm laughing at. Silly old crone, I'm thinking, go back to your ridiculous old life. But the sidewalks are lumpy in that neighborhood and I'm not used to such high heels. Just as I pass her, I trip and twist my ankle, and there I am on the dirty sidewalk. She's looking me right in the eye, and I see it *is* my old other self indeed, or might as well be. I can see disapproval of my costume in her eyes, disapproval of my whole being, in fact, but the feeling is mutual. She reaches out her hand to help me up. I grab it, jerk hard, and pull her down beside me. Then, leaning on her shoulder, I get up and try my foot. It still hurts, but maybe it's just one of those strains that hurt a lot at the beginning and go away in three or four minutes.

I hop away from her. She looks as if she doesn't know what's happening, but *I* do. And she seems to me to have deteriorated into a hopeless mass of jelly that might as well be left oozing on the sidewalk—though, as usual, I'm full of contradictory impulses. I pulled the old lady down, yes, but I have a lot of sympathy for her once she's getting dirty there on the sidewalk. Suddenly I have the thought to lift her up, let her go on her way, safe and sound, and leave myself lying there alone. I do know exactly how she feels. I even have a momentary sense of confusion myself as if *I* was the one who wonders what's happening. I almost do, in fact, give her a helping hand. Yes, yes, I might have done it if it wasn't for the pain in my foot. I have had, all along, a special warm feeling for her — except, on the other hand, I want her feeling helpless and, most particularly, abandoned. So let some other old lady pick her up. I limp away. I will limp away and take a taxi. I can afford it.

Back home, I decide to spend the next few days in bed reading *The Realities of Fantasy.* Then, later, back at work at the library, I will, once and for all, dispose of the card for the book called *Capturing Desire*.

Basically, I'm pleased with myself. Yes, this is not to be taken as a failure, but as a first try. And he said it himself, Marshal:

> Oh, the persistence of desire! Whether a suitable desire or not, one must not limit oneself, neither to the practical nor the impractical, neither to the suitable nor the unsuitable, and one must certainly realize that it is the unsuitable desire that always touches us the most deeply.

Mental Health and Its Alternative

If only I could define myself in terms of my up-days, all the curves of my graph rising at the same time and staying up for more than a couple of hours. And if only I could feel that I was I at more than just those few exhilarating moments, how my breasts would loom and swell up into the landscape and his hand (spontaneously) — or yours, even — would come into view across my stomach, and another hand under my head or under my buttocks, I suppose. I'd call it fortunate if such a thing could be."The King Kong of cows and finally," I'd say (or "again") though actually a *small* King Kong Queen of Cow (K.K.Q. of C.) — however no really right way to be a woman that I can find at this particular time.

"Feel free to exist anyhow," the psychologist says. Fear of heights makes him grab for his crotch.

"Oh, if only I could, I would like to end up with a little bit of both sexes: status, comfort, and compliance! Brute force! Surrender! Be a mystery *and* a big-shot!"

Yes, the legendary Doctor Sanglant will fulfill all expectations. He has said it (but forgot to tell me expectations change). Looking down his delicate nose (his best feature) he has already told me I will one day write exquisitely, or at the very least, much faster. He wears a top hat, white tie, etc., and as I enter the office, he throws a little piece of lighted flash paper while I open a can labeled "Mixed Nuts" and out pops a long, green snakey, spring-thing.

"Pick a card. Any card."

I hide behind my hair, my glasses, my thumb and two fingers. I cross and recross my legs to create a diversion, but it may turn out I will no longer have to choose the Queen of Swords now that I have dreamt King Kong Cow.

"I dreamed," I tell him, "that you stuck your little finger in my ear and then put it up your nose."

Doctor Sachlich jots that down. I try to sneak a look, but he plays his cards close to his chest.

So far, there's no blood on me. It's all on Doctor Sangfroid's dress-shirt front: the only splash, or rather drip, of color. It comes from a small stab wound I have inadvertently inflicted in his side (or was it yours?). I yell, "Don't hurt me. I'm helpless!" Doctor Sanglot sighs and keeps silent, nonintervention his best policy. Agony is mine and always has been, because if I should, by some mistake, show joy, someone might think I was happy and do nothing for me.

The stab wound is a Jesus-wound, as in the paintings: one cool, clean trickle of blood from probably just the screwdriver part of a small jackknife. It can't have done much harm, and as a matter of fact, Doctor Sangriento tells me that so far, I have been doing exactly what my type of neurotic always does. I'm glad. I always wanted to do the customary thing, though to be truthful, I have conflicting feelings about this. On the one hand, yes, to know the norm so as to achieve it: the criteria, that is, for proper behavior, legitimate bliss, orthodox ecstasy, customary bed-mates, sanitary raptures with suitable objects of desire. . . . But, on the other hand, I want the dazzle of forbidden mysteries: hypnosis, trances, LSD! Legendary lust behind the psychoanalytic doors. I want to know all the private, lecherous details of the other patients' lives, knowledge of the psychologist's secret vices, plus totally new and (especially) unimaginable positions for it. I want to live, giddy, at the edge of abandonment (and yet somehow still be in the 92 percent of everybody, or the 56 percent, if only that). He has said, "Pick a card," but I want the whole deck.

And I do pick one, but I don't let him see it. This time I escape attention by telling him about King Kong Cow who is black and white or all-over tan and fatter than a gorilla, would not climb the Empire State Building nor take women away, except to some better land; would perform, if asked, willingly for the stardom of it and to see herself on TV. "Great Cow, I mean Great Primordial Cow," I say, "was once queen of everything, or some like to think so. She has thirteen breasts. Seven virgins suck there, the milk of the sweet sense of (female) self." Really it's four hundred breasts and four hundred virgins, but I don't want to boast.

And now I have already gone home and come back a week later in an entirely different mood and Doctor Sanguiferous has a little clown-smile painted over his lips. He wears a paper party hat. It's a blue-and-white, deja-vu hat because I already dreamt he would have one like that. I can see in his eyes that he is laughing at me. That makes sense. Especially since I don't remember a single thing he said to me last time nor what I said to him.

"Pick a card. Pick a card." And I do, but this time he won't let *me* see it. I neither get to see my own card nor a glimpse of depravity.

This time I had tried to make a grand entrance, throwing my red scarf back over my shoulder (and I'm wearing boots, too), but I had slipped on a small, black smudge, probably a raisin. (Perhaps one of my own since I'm into health food. Perhaps, though, one of his, deliberately put there to trip me up.) Next I had tried for a passable (at least) preliminary gesture. I wanted to do something right, but I realize now that I must get adjusted to the full alphabet of myself, up to *F* for failure, up to *I* for incomplete. (I will probably walk out with his raisin stuck to my boot.)

"Struggle on," I *thought* I heard him say, "with your ridiculous, inept, exaggerated, far-fetched and overly emotional, female-type thoughts, Dumb Broad." Why he's Daddy, Freud, Houdini, and society-in-general all rolled into one! I see that now, and now I have heard *it*—those very words that seem to lie unsaid behind so much of what is said—have heard it, or thought I heard it, from his own lips. The basic truth at last and at this price, or cheap at any. I decide I like his little painted-on, V-shaped smile. I try to smile one like it for my own cross-purposes, no longer feeling like Queen King Kong, but rather more (sitting squirming here) Queen of the termites and visible, damn it! This chair (but I already knew that) for feeling uncomfortable in. It has a broken spring that, as I try to wriggle away, catches on my buttocks. It's the pain that makes me cry. I wipe my tears on my blindfold.

I tell him that I have already broken seven mirrors.

I tell him I have changed all the names in order to protect the guilty.

I tell him (and I dreamt this) that the cunt is a silk purse made out of a sow's ear.

I tell him that I have been locked in so many trunks with false bottoms. That the keys to the handcuffs were put between my teeth as in all the symbolic movies, but that I forgot they were there and I swallowed them. "Perhaps I could have recovered them later, on a menstrual pad," I say, "if I had thought to look, but that only occurred to me right this very minute."

"There are drinks," Doctor Sans Pareille says, "that can make you seem to fly or change sizes or feel sexy or see everything as though from under water. There's poison mushrooms and toad's juice . . ."

But I'm not listening.

The psychologist of the happy is a happy psychologist. He laughs all day and only cries from too much laughing. When he has a picnic at the beach for all his patients they let loose caged birds along with helium balloons, and after that they breathe the helium and talk in squeaky voices, and when suddenly the sun comes out (if it wasn't already), all the patients turn cartwheels in the sand and play psychological pranks and do all sorts of psychological shenanigans. They are relating to each other like a bunch of psychotherapists at their annual August Psychoanalytic conference, winking and hugging each other. They are gazing deep into each other's eyes, patting each other's shoulders, rubbing the backs of each other's necks, and to them, the seagulls are sounding soft as doves. (Caws, quacks, and screeches, on the other hand, follow me wherever I go and a lot of those sounds I make myself.)

Doctor Sans Souci is getting his patients all mixed up. Now he thinks *I'm* the one who never had an orgasm. What folly! And now he thinks I'm the one who's trying to adjust to having only one breast. "Talk about it. Try," he says.

"About what?"

But perhaps he means breasts and orgasms figuratively speaking.

I had rehearsed the telling of a very long dream, but I decide, out of spite, not to tell it. He is, I see it now, only partially omnipotent.

"Women," he says, "they're all losers, still looking for living space in the living room."

He is breathing down my neck. My back is against the wall. (The jaws of my womb have already snapped shut. I can feel it at the base of my spine.) He has just made a claustrophobic gesture. I stare at the floor pretending not to notice. Which of us is winning so far, I wonder—you, him, or me? . . . Daddy, Houdini, Freud, or society-in-general?

Now when they shout "Camera! Action!" all I can say is, What's the plot? Not wanting any of the same old stories, and anyway, I don't like it . . . to be left stumbling here as Queen King Kong of Cow crushing kittens . . . I mean kitchens and the little phony buildings of a toy Tokyo as if it mattered, dragging my udders over bridges and no-man's land and a man's hand sometimes, and me doing more harm to myself than to any of "them." "If only she could have used her power for good," they keep saying, "instead of *talking* so much." But how does K.K.Q. of C use . . . I mean milk and eggs and mother's mooing? And it's always some man choreographs the cow-trip through the city. Oh, anyway, I love the look in his eyes, the choreographer's. I'll let him overpower me easily despite my size. This man has got to be *crazy* . . . (I mean about me) and I know what crazy is.

But what's the logic of holding on to some poor male in my big fist like this? He's balding, paunchy, forgetful and preoccupied (though not with me), sweating, busy, has cancerous lumps on the skin of his face and sometimes gets out of breath right in the middle of making love. (I forgive him some of these things.) But my hands, I suppose, clutch at whatever drowning man I can reach at any given time.

Queen Cow sighs . . . is sighing again. "It's birth order," she says (having, for the moment, forgotten all about her older half-sister), "the crux of the whole thing."

"If only you could have used your power for good," he says, "instead of in the service of ambivalence." I answer with a soft mooing which he takes for a groan. "Drink this," he says, "and come nearer to perfection."

She is already salivating at the sight of his little bell.

"You will need a temporary love-brace and perhaps some special devices, all electronic, or simply two candles. You will need kisses across each clavicle. You will need to let your fingers play around in somebody else's pubic hair and vice versa. You will need both hands on your man, your lips on his nipple. You will also need changes in a flash, Shazam! or in a shower of sparks! But meanwhile I will give you," he says, "three wishes."

But he has looked into my one good eye and suddenly stopped talking.

"I need," I say, "I need, but all I ever get is to cavort along the sidelines, though tricks and sometimes treats."

"Ah," he says, "now you're finally catching on, but that's a somewhat different topic. It was, *some* say," he says, "for the sake of an old woman that the Aztec cut out a million, or rather, millions of hearts and also sometimes sucked away the brains. The human equivalent of the cosmic . . . just what you're talking about—tricks or treats, that is—that make some kind of sense out of the universe through the female . . . ."

But I can't stand it! I can't stand it! Being of the sex that's responsible for everything sensual or morbid or for those sacred, deadly ball games. Us—get this! me, even—the overturned vessel of doom or standing as a symbol for it! I don't want to be an archetype. I will send Doctor Sangria a notice to that effect as follows:

NOTICE OF DETERMINATION OF TERMINATION

It is ordered, that as of the date of this order, I, King Kong Queen of Cow, no longer shall be thought of as Great Round, Earth Mother, Big Mama; nor Grandmother Spider, nor moon, nor moon-cat; nor, as they call it, "inert, primeval watery mass;" nor western devourer who eats her own children; nor three fates, nor three witches; nor weaver, miller; nor oven of transformations, no; nor in any way connected with intoxicants, nor bringer of intoxication and/or death, as the bringer of life also brings death, I, Queen King Kong Cosmic Cow, not to be considered or confused with anything sacred nor anything fearsome; nor, therefore, with flood or hurricane, nor stand as a symbol for it; nor mother of all the gods, nor of any of the gods, and not even responsible for the conception of a baby more than any man is, no; nor for the luring of the opposite sex into traps of licentiousness, no; nor stand for it in any form—whether wearing a bra or not—not now nor ever stand for it; nor the maw of the earth nor engulfing womb; nor accept any still-beating hearts of warriors, nor devour umbilical cords; nor stroke the heads of cobras, nor any other creature of dread; nor tiger's tongue in my mouth, nor stand for any such thing as a symbol of it, not now and forever, no.

Standing—one leg up, the other bent at the knee—in the pose of a whelping bitch—so as to confirm, for all to see, my sex (is it ugly?) — as in an ancient statue there was once of Queen Cow posed in this same half-sitting position, as the mother of even the very first of the gods or as, on the other hand, the overturned vessel of doom — what hand, at such a time as this, dares touch my udders? What hand other than my own golden hand as I, posed here as though it were New York, head facing the twin towers, I, yearning, as usual, self-vindicating cosmic cow, being touched by . . . what hand, damn it, but *your* hand! Touch the udder, the golden underside of it, other hand at velvet nose. Cow's eyes look out at, damn it, *you*! How, now, not see, when sometimes even Doctor Sagenhaft has to turn away from my gaze? Why, now, you do it too?

"A raging cow," Doctor Sache says, "does not become a bull." He is trying to keep a straight face. I dare not speak again, especially not with words like: *numinous* or *luminous*, *nimbus*, *scintillation*, or any others like them. And as of this moment, I suspect Doctor Sangrar of everything and anything, and you too, and Daddy and Freud.

And now I have already gone home and come back and come back and gone home and come back and Doctor Sanguine, humming to himself, has again offered me those same three wishes of which I have, so far, accepted only two so as to have the last one saved for later. The Doctor is actually singing! I can't believe it. You would almost think he is the psychoanalyst of the happy, or at the very least, of the mostly sane today. He is reshuffling all his cards and has plucked a silver dollar out of my ear, but sleight-of-hand (I know that by now) is only slightly magic.

The last time I stuttered it was on the word *sex*.

And now I have already gone home and come back and come back and gone home three times again and I have almost called my own bluff.

If Doctor Santé had wanted to, he could have told me all about myself at the very first session, but I think it's too late now that he has shrunk to almost normal size, and I can see that he has, after all, problems of his own.

But wait! Change! Yes — a sudden change, bliss (or almost) and not a moment too soon, either, though I know it's only temporary. Doctor Songster, foot on desk, hardly cracks a smile at my ridiculous pirouette.

To you, then, who are about to give . . . I mean to take, that is, up dancing or something somewhat similar according to your special needs and tastes and talents, having put yourselves into the hands of an experienced master, you ought to know that theory alone will not suffice. To acquire the necessary equilibrium . . . to be found (having jumped, for a moment, UP) . . . to be found in the right position while actually in midair! Not grace, exactly, but some kind of mastery of movement and time, having dispensed, once and for all, with embellishments, divested of all elegance . . . (all the mirrors having been turned to the walls) . . . To you, then, who, having put yourself in good hands and about to leap and perhaps dance and/or to forget as well as to remember and in order to perceive the pleasures of it, to give in and take (in or out), and to take part in, I mean to you . . . to you who are about to, Doctor Song has sung. Doctor Sang is singing . . . .

But now it's already several years later and the above ending is already not the kind of ending that's coming true. The future is less known, in fact, than ever, and I am aware that perhaps the Doctor has not been sitting there in silent judgement all this time. And perhaps there actually is no right position to be found while in midair, as well as no right way to begin. Simply to be in midair will suffice. Simply to begin.

The Promise of Undying Love

We have always yearned for great men. We have been impressed by them. In fact, dazzled! Spellbound! We have even hoped to have a truly great man of our own one day. Dressed in our best, we have gone where great men go, where they cluster in groups of greatness. We have watched them from the balcony of the Senate as well as from the balconies of theaters and concert halls. Watched them on TV. We have sat in their classes and agreed with them desperately. We have waited for them outside stage doors, sent them admiring letters, called them up. We have always felt that the achieving of an achieving man was worth any amount of pain and trouble and we have taken pains and trouble and suffered untold hardships. And sometimes we have concentrated so hard on great men that the great men themselves have seen our interest in our eyes. And this has paid off occasionally, and some of us have had, at least for a little while, the company of a great—or more likely a "near-great"—man. But usually our attempts to contact the great and near-great fail and we have to turn to ordinary men. Certainly this is true in the long run. After we have lost most of our good looks, that is. Our needs, however, are even greater then, but we have less hope of satisfying them and so we have to take what is available. Have to kiss lesser cheeks, lesser lips; make do with less money; have to choose the larger and/or most beautiful of two or three lesser penises.

(Often, for want of a great man, we have pushed our sons toward greatness as best we could.)

But can one exist—that is the question—can one exist without a great man? One is alive, that's about all. One goes about one's business trapped in the everyday. No sparkle and (especially) no glory.

We have resolved that this should no longer be true, that none of us should have to live this kind of half-life. Now we will bring great men down among us. We will entertain them in informal ways and treat them — be allowed to treat them — almost like we treat everyone else: kiss them and hold hands, pinch them, tickle them, lean on their arm, slap and giggle — but not anymore just *any* great man. We want the greatest! That he should be here with us. That we could, should the occasion warrant it, slap, giggle, tickle and pinch the greatest man of all.

As mentioned, most attempts to contact great and near-great end in failure or, at best, achieve only a short-term success. How much more difficult, then, to contact and capture the greatest man of all, but how much more rewarding, too. Certainly he is worth any journey: by mule, by foot, by plane, by rubber raft . . . . And so we will track down, trip-up, seduce, fall upon, or fall down in front of, now, even the very greatest man of them all.

He has been hidden away from us. Guards and dogs have kept us from him. A few women have entered his citadel from time to time, but soon came out too broken — probably by the simple fact of having to leave him and to leave the citadel — too broken to speak of it. Afterwards they lead sad lives. Lately the great man has been kept so hidden that it has been necessary for us to find ways of confirming his existence. Chances are, we found, that he *is* still alive and well (according to the laws of probability if nothing else). And we have seen pictures of him through a windshield or a window; we have seen a hand on a doorknob; and once on TV through a telephoto lens, we have seen a huge dark, and fully clothed figure striking poses on the beach.

But our most recent researches have shown a startling fact. Though no one will admit it, the great man has, we think, already disappeared. Even the other great men don't know exactly where he has gone or why. But we wonder how can this be? That a man of such magnificent size and with such a voice as his, that a man of such a temperament as we have heard his is . . . How could such a man quietly vanish?

There is an important clue to his possible whereabouts. The great man had been known to say on numerous occasions that he wanted to find a warm valley or the breezy top of a mountain or that he wanted to recover from a long illness and be nursed back to health by strangers; that he wanted to wake up with total amnesia, wanted to parachute from a plane into a jungle or be washed up on a foreign shore. In short, wanted to rise up new and fresh without all the old bad habits, the old tics and grimaces. And who among us, man or woman, hasn't wished the same, including crash-landing (safely) on another planet?

Now we must put ourselves in the same position: strike out blindly into forests, crash-land on islands, be washed up on some shore or other.

Except we must be wary. There will certainly be impostors, many of them may be almost as large as the great man himself, and wearing the same rumpled brown suits, brutal and morose, sad and selfish . . . . Also many of these men may follow the same procedures the great man does in the making of the monumental, may spend their time in foundries or on scaffolding, huge sketches lining their walls. They may stare out of top-story windows for hours. We must not inadvertently fall in love with some slightly lesser version of the man.

One of the questions that comes instantly to mind, of course, is: Will we be able to get along with, or be happy with, a man of this sort, being as we are, of an entirely different cast of mind? But the question is absurd because we never expected the great to be easy to live with. We know the great are selfish (how could they have become so great without that?) and we're ready for it and willing to put up with it. And, in fact, trained for this from the very beginning. We have been taught to put up with almost anything for the other advantages, but mainly that our love will have found an object worthy of it. The great are, we believe, worth even the sacrifice of our own happiness.

We have a dossier with several photographs of the greatest man of all at several different stages of his life and in several different situations, and we have a list of moles, scars, tics and mannerisms. After having studied this dossier closely for a long time, I was in love with the greatest man already. Also with his moles, scars, tics, etc. Already even (or especially) his faults (the crooked teeth, for instance) are "adorable" to me. Already I feel empty without him. Historians of love—and there have been more than one might think—historians of love (and Stendhal in particular) said: "The most surprising thing of all about love is the first step," and here I have already taken it, am already greedy for the great man's praise. We all are. We all wake up calling out to him from our dreams. And we are, all of us, hoping that he will say to us one day: "Love, let us be true to one another," etc. . . . And we hope he will be, at last, true, though that is not his reputation.

I must be tested, tempered by fire and ice, adventures, trials, hardships. Years must pass until I find myself at this age I am right now and exactly at this stage, no longer beautiful (if ever) but in a different kind of prime than just good looks: a wiry, rugged, thin, and sunburned prime. I have returned again and again to and through towns, cities, forests, islands . . . . At last I come upon another teeming shore with another symbolic leaky boat, without oars, pulled up beyond the tide line, another flight of vast stone steps, another avenue with cherry trees in bloom. But I have lost all interest in these externals, and lately (and for the first time in my life, actually), I have even been trying to imagine what life *without* the great man would be like. Probably pay attention, then, only to simple details, and of course, no longer need much money if no great man in the offing. No need to spend it on preparing myself for him and no need to spend it on searching for him. Not, anymore, try to hide my wrinkles. Let myself get fat. Perhaps after all these years be cured of my love and longings, right here, several feet from the east face; and yet, on the other hand, might turn the corner, mount the steps and there he might be at last . . . all of sixty-five or seventy by now. And now, I . . . having already mounted the steps, not, of course, to see the president himself, but to see the man behind the president. *Not* figuratively speaking, but the man who is standing behind the president right now, here to unveil his largest and most monumental work. He has been, it is clear, in plain sight all the while. Only gone off for a short vacation and come back long ago, no doubt while I was cracked up in the jungle or scrambling around on top of some mountain and didn't hear about it.

All my life so far has been a preparation for this moment, but now, when it comes right down to it, I have no plan or procedure. I have not taken time out from the search nor from the preparation of myself as desirable object to get ready for the actual confrontation. What's more, I stand here improperly dressed. I stand here dirty and tired and, and most unfortunate, unfeminine. What to do? What to say? (First, perhaps let a few tears streak my dusty face.)

And suddenly the words do pour out. "You see me," I say, "not as I was, but what *you've* made me. If I have sacrificed my beauty and the best years of my life (and I have) it has been for *your* sake. *You* did this to me. What I am now, nothing but skin and bone and muscle, is all *your* fault."

But is this the way to a healthy relationship? And can it be that we are already quarreling or about to (depending on what he will say)? I can't anticipate my own next words. Perhaps I should try to stop talking if only for a moment.

I have a view of his crotch from here, where I stand below him on the steps. The thighs are huge. The brown pants sag, especially just there, at the center. It is the crotch at eye level that I have been speaking to. I do not dare speak to the eyes. When I look at them I see that he is a failure, or at least *he* thinks so. And these steps. They are not the steps of the capitol building and not even those of the cultural center, but other, lesser steps, though almost as long and though they have that same sort of look about them.

I have no sympathy for him. After all, if he is a failure, then I, too, have failed.

But suddenly I remember that I have a message from all of us. "We all," I say, "we all . . . we all . . . we *all*. . . ." The word "love" does not come easily to my lips. Perhaps I have held it in too long, always thinking about it, yes, but never saying it . . . never finding anyone worthy of it. It is stuck in my throat. Perhaps I will choke on the word "love." But then, before I can stop myself, I am back on the former topic, as though *instead* of love. "You must do something for me," I say, "because, though I haven't met you until now, I have been deeply wronged by you already." (How can we get better acquainted if I keep reiterating this complaint?)

But how not speak out? This man could have changed my life any time he wanted to, simply by coming into view. Is that too much to ask? Why has he kept himself away until he, too, has grown old—until he, clearly, is not the greatest man of *this* decade? Still, by now I'm too tired to care. This great man will have to do. I, like all except a very few women, will make do . . . always making do with what's at hand.

For want of a better idea, then, and partially in order to stop the flow of my own words, I fall at his feet. I hope into a small and desirable bundle. I'm thinking that whatever happens now will certainly change my life.

He comes daintily down the next few steps. Lifts me up. (I will let myself be taken anywhere.) He limps, he shuffles with me in his soft, fat arms, on down and out to the beach not far beyond. I'm thinking: How about if we *both* drift out in a boat with no oars? How about the two of us washed up on some shore? How about both of us with amnesia or terribly high fevers found by the natives of a lovely valley or of another planet? But perhaps there is a place where the great go at this time in their lives. Let him take me there. Let him take me where he will. I'm tired of thinking for myself.

(I'm guessing that he knows what I know — that he has finally met the woman meant for him — because in his eyes the lost dog look.)

But he is carrying me on past the boat. "No, no," I shout. "The boat. Put me in the boat." He turns around, a glimmer of hope on his face and starts to put me in it. "Silly man," I say, "push off first," and he puts me down and does, the surf washing at his pant legs. Then he puts me in and seems to think to turn me loose in the waves alone, but I won't let go. I have a good grip on his lapel with one hand and on his beard with the other. He struggles. He is leaning on the gunnels and I am too near the edge myself. The boat teeters sideways and then goes over, hitting him on the head and knocking us both into the waves.

I rescue him. Large as he is, I pull him up on shore. (It's a good thing I've had all these years of hardships to tone my muscles and hone my quick reactions.) I lie down beside him, in my rightful place at last. If I'm lucky, perhaps when he wakes up he will not remember anything. Here, in each other's arms, we will have a new beginning. Perhaps this is our foreign shore already. It is to be hoped.

"I forgive you," I whisper in his ear. "I forgive you everything that's happened so far."

There Is No God But Bog

This little design represents the hundred thousand eyes of Bog:

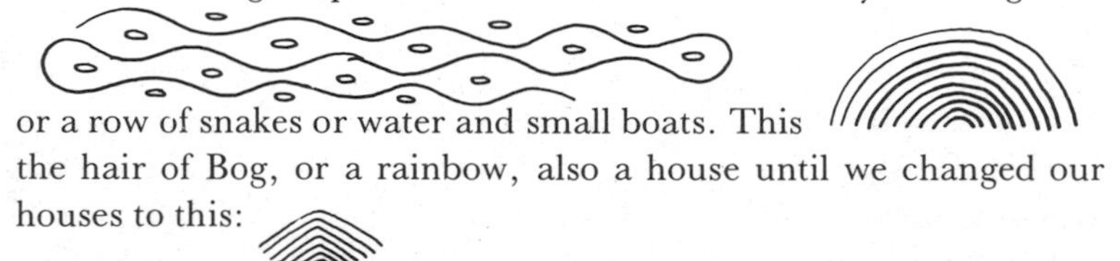

or a row of snakes or water and small boats. This the hair of Bog, or a rainbow, also a house until we changed our houses to this:

This next, the busy fingers of Bog or two large combs stuck together:

Sometimes a river. The color of Bog's eyes is all color, therefore white. His body is no color, therefore black. He comes from outer space.

If one little man should try to make himself understood by Bog he should wonder, Does anybody notice one ant more than another? Robert ate for four for seven years and grew enormous in order to be understood by Bog. Howard formed words out of trees (some a thousand years old) and set fire to them in order to be understood by Bog. Edgar, at age twelve, castrated himself with his mother's paring knife and learned to sing the sweetest songs in hopes that Bog would hear him. John jumped out of a building, hoping to be understood by Bog on the way down, if only for a few seconds.

One thousand eyes are as one eye and this is a one-eyed man or Bog's box:

It is the media center for being understood by Bog. It frequently breaks down and the link to the airways is severed, so that if seven virgins sing, the sound is not heard beyond the immediate vicinity.

How innocent Bog looks seen through the wrong end of a telescope thus: How he does fool us with sailboats on a sparkling sea; with house plants; with smooth, round stones; and, now and then, a waterfall!

He made the ozone. He set it about the earth as a protection for us. It took years of preparation. He could let it stay there if he really wanted to.

Pray for the ozone.

If Bog wanted to play the banjo, he could do it just like that, without a single lesson.

We don't need him quite so much now that we found out about vitamin C.

"Make me laugh or cry," he says, and we do, and then we say "Make *us* laugh or cry," and he does. But then, when he says, "One, two, three, you're dead," we are suddenly full of self-doubt.

Here is a diagram of the ups, the downs, and the level places of the three main cycles (menstrual, biorhythm, and barometer) for one month (or whatever passes for a month). It is also lips about to smile, or a spider, or an N within an M:

This is Bog, sideways (we are *not* in his image):

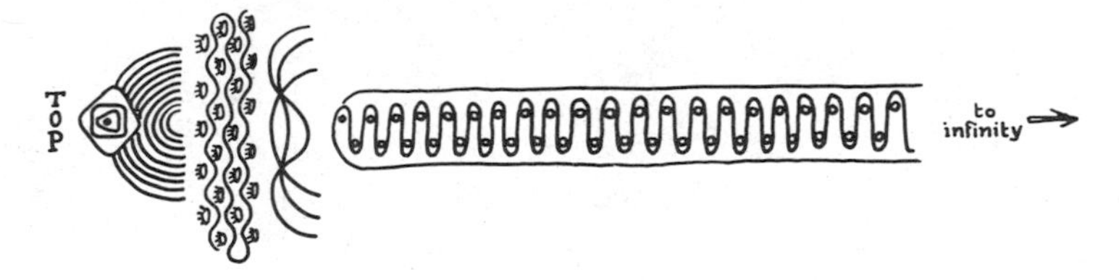

He is sometimes found in full regalia, dancing on the head of a pin.

He is a self-made god. He took the initiative, and of his own accord, decided: Let there be one great big explosion, and there was, and he saw that it was good.

Pray that, in the twinkling of an eye, one quarter of the world's population should be turned into trees. Also, and in another twinkling, there should be three more abortion clinics right here in New York City. Let it be that two thousand women who have missed their periods, and who tremble at the very thought, should sigh with relief less than two weeks from right now. Let there be about half as many houses around the cities as now, and let *my* house disappear and me also, if need be; and let me become a ponderosa pine of about the same age as I am now and let me stand in the corner of this very plot overlooking the garden. And let some of these new trees be from men who would have committed the murder of good men and let the good men come and stand in their shade. And others should be of those people who want to die anyway so that this will give them a good and pain-free sort of life. And some will be of the mothers who are cruel to their children. It is better to be a tree. But, assuming that one quarter of the world's population can't be all bad, then some will have to be good people of small means and little education.

And while you're at it, give us not this day so much daily bread, but give some of it to the Africans so that they may live and that we may go about the land lean and willowy as we were meant to do. Let the traffic be up to the speed limit every day of our lives, though not above it. Let three thousand more blacks suddenly get top jobs in management. Let not the sewage pollute the seas nor industrial waste take over our lands. And that day when the boiling rain falls and the sidewalks rise up under our feet, when buildings topple and the air explodes in our lungs; the jaw hangs unhinged, the eardrums burst, the eyes pop out and we are caught, innocently, in some huge blast — then hold our blown-up hands in thine just once before we are completely zapped.

One little nobody with small breasts and two or three children . . . . How can he even be equipped to understand her and her little problems of what she might consider right or wrong? Even though his big, white, red-rimmed eyes are everywhere, transparent as the see-through air, not everybody is worthy of notice. And some say god makes only monumental decisions — those, for instance, that involve the slow movement of the different political divisions of land away from the single great land mass, Pangaea (which he thought of first, but has, it seems, rejected). It's

Pangaea (which he thought of first, but has, it seems, rejected). It's slow work, but in this age of rapid transportation and communication this separation is even more desirable than it might have been before, if only for a few more seconds of privacy. And so some oceans shrink while others take up the slack. Land masses slip sideways by inches every year. With that and with the planet's wobble, we are dizzy almost all the time and roll as we walk and feel queasy when we look up into the sky.

Anxious to please and to be pleased, Bog gave us sex. Bog loves life with love and sex in it. You can tell by all the goings on among the birds and the bees, the worms, the flowers . . . the passers-by, headwaiters, salesmen, people seen out of train windows, men of letters, men of action—and women too—even the most level-headed of them. Bog said, "Let there be sex," and there was, and a lot of it, especially on the night side, and every creature had a lot of fun and had babies and the mothers turned as playful as their children and cooed and kissed. Girls were even named for the sex organs of plants, such as Lily, Rose, and Daisy. It turned out to be a game where everybody wins and Bog didn't mind that. He saw that it was good and (usually) in the public interest.

This is the symbol for sex: 

As is self-evident, it is two monthly ups and downs combined in one figure. Also, as is self-evident, it is the penis seen head on
and the vulva:

There is a kind of wispy nothingness all around us that, if it were gathered into one place, would hardly fill an ordinary picnic basket. That is the stuff of Bog. The teachers of touching say it has no feel at all, but if we think somebody strokes our cheeks sometimes in the evenings, that's it, brushing by.

(Silence is like that, too; sometimes we hear it whispering in our ears. That, also, is Bog.)

Having been touched and standing in that heavenly light making appropriate gestures . . . . Are we more likely to succeed after these ceremonials?

Sometimes, while expecting assistance and protection, we get nothing but bad weather. Sometimes he seems to favor slugs and toadstools over any of us.

Innocent people drown every summer. Don't ask why.

He is a nonconforming, avant-garde god, inventive and playful. Witness the giraffe, the platypus, plants that bloom only once in four years, the ginkgo tree (and the word for it), peacocks, the sexual practices of the snail . . . . Get out from under your roofs and up on a hill or a tall building for an uncluttered view of the sky. Look! Out in the milky way and beyond, there are nothing but absurdities . . . a lot of crazy stars without—get this—hardly any pattern at all, simply strewn all over the sky every which way. One can hardly find a dipper, dragon or swan in a dozen of them. Sometimes the universe looks a lot like the top of my coffee table, completely out of control, or so it seems from down here. More cautious gods might at least have checked the lay of the sky before tossing things out so rashly. Who knows but what, later on, Bog may vote no to the whole bit in one final paroxysm of disgust, or out of carelessness, or simply because the whole thing's no fun anymore.

Entropy does *not* mean that the fire and fight have gone out of him.

Bog's penises: 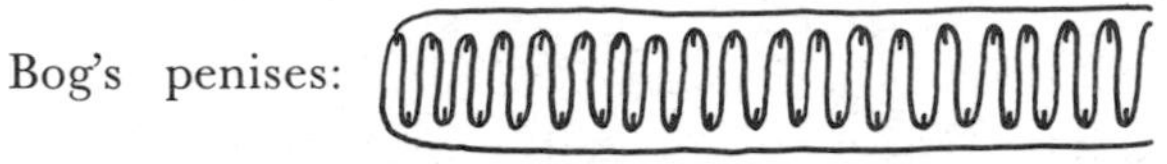 to infinity.

Don't laugh or think that's wrong. It has to be that way. But being both eschatological and scatological, he will be the least of all to be censorious. What he wants is to be laughed at sometimes with a wink or leer, and other times he likes both arms upraised to the heavens and a shout or a good song about himself, but mostly he wants to be believed in.

Bad news: You will all die.

But smile. Make a joyful noise unto Bog and do not think: How could this be! And so suddenly! It could, it could. (Did you look in your tea leaves?) Even if you've done many miscellaneous holy acts, it happens.

He is responsible for the lollipops, combs, pens, calendars (especially those), the tiny boxes of laundry flakes, and all the other free things including the air. He himself may be a kind of something extra, a sort of lagniappe of the universe (as if there wasn't enough already even without him).

How he sometimes gets his kicks: "I will offer thee three;" he says (in Second Samuel), "choose thee one of them, that I may do it unto thee." Enemies, famines, floods, and/or pestilences. Locusts may come. Other things might happen in subways or unlit vestibules. (Once, my car keys fell into a street drain just when I was about to hurry home.)

I bite my finger as hard as I can if I find myself thinking agnostic thoughts.

But not *too* hard because sometimes a lesson can be so painful to learn that one forgets it as soon as one can.

Bless us and bless our gross national product. Let our brakes hold and our gas be plentiful. Let us also find alternate sources of energy. And let the world keep twirling and the sun last in its present form as long as you can possibly manage it.

But to him, actually, one silly solar system must seem much like another.

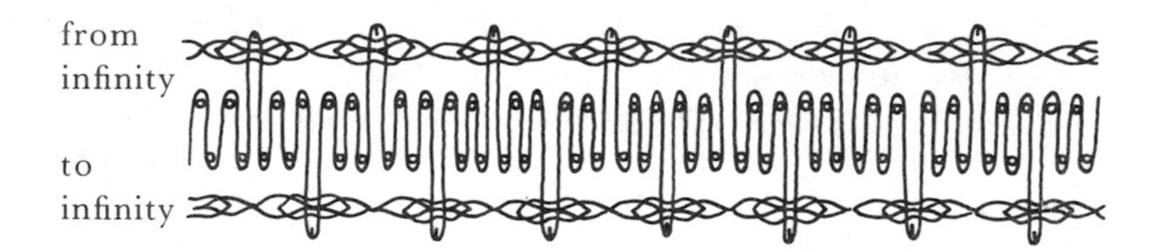

Expecting Sunshine and Getting It

SUDDENLY I DO NOT UNDERESTIMATE MYSELF.

I think *I* am probably the dark, brooding stranger, riding a wild horse that only *I* can control and followed by big, dangerous dogs. I think *I* am most likely the person returning from long voyages in strange lands, knowing many esoteric languages and customs and having left children (God knows where or who knows who their fathers are) in several of those countries. (Could I really do that?) I think that *I* am probably the romantic, eligible bachelor-woman; rich, of course, and waiting for the right man — the mousy man in brown who takes off his glasses — who'll tame me. I shout at a raucous shout. I shout that he's frightened my horse, etc. My first impression is of the kind of nondescript male who should keep out of my way. But I have surprised horses myself every now and then as they came out of the mist when I happened to be standing there yelling and waving my arms, and now I have surprised even myself, my cloak flying as I ride in storms, wet and not caring and regardless of the menopause. Thunder roars.

I'm thinking that *I* must be the one who lives in the castle. Kafka (all in brown) watches from the village below, but I'm the one with the haunted eyes. I can't help that. I probably have several secret sorrows, not the least of which is that I already have a husband locked up in the tower. Sometimes you can hear his crazy laughing, though what has he got to laugh about? (Kafka believes in one husband at a time, that's clear, but I have my fantasies.)

If I should ever yell "cunt" or "dildo" in one of my rages I can be pretty sure K never heard those words before. That's one kind of high class I'm after, now that I can try for nothing but the best.

I drive past him fast several times a day. I keep circling back. There's danger probably reflected in my dark glasses and they flash back at him (along with my signals), a glimpse of his own mousy face. (He always said he hated the sight of it. I remember reading that someplace.) If he doesn't catch on for himself soon, I will have to get somebody to tell him that I might be, or might not be, from the castle. I will have to have someone tell him that I might suddenly go off on another long journey. Time is short. How long can this mood last?

Here are the facts: The storm came out of the North and I probably came with it. My rage was such that I forgot my sagging breasts, my aging face, my varicosities, arthritis, etc., etc. I didn't scream, "I'm not crazy, I'm not crazy," by then and it was probably no longer a question of just setting fire to the bedsheets. At that moment, risking everything (except, of course, the children), feeling I had the strength of ten (and I guess I did), I locked Mr. Rochester in the tower room and he's the one who's laughing out the window now, not me.

I was his first love, remember that? For all anyone knows, I may have been an orphan, too, and not necessarily have had a happy childhood. We know I had a brother. Probably he was given all the education even though I might have been smarter. Anyway, I did all right up to a certain point in spite of everything, but so many good things hadn't been invented yet and of course I never knew when he'd come home or whether he'd come home at all. He was that kind of man. (Had there been telephones, he wouldn't have called.) Sexual techniques were primitive. It wasn't even a question of clitoral or vaginal. By four o'clock every afternoon I was already yelling at the children and watching the clock for no good reason since what could happen? Maybe if we'd lived in the city instead of the suburbs. Maybe if we'd gone for professional help in time, but it's too late for that now. Anyway, that's all changed and sometimes after riding around all day trying to catch K's eye, I climb the tower stairs and let Mr. Rochester groan and shake his Orson Wellesish head at me. I let him plead and bitch and squeeze out a few tears like I used to do, and if it looks OK, I open the bars like he used to do for me and we make crazy, mad, violent, psychopathic love. The best kind. And then I leave quickly before he gets the upper hand. (It's nice, sometimes, to have a man all your own, one that you're not trying to impress anymore, or influence or plead with.)

He says it's not fair, but fairness is my specialty and always has been. It's what I've yearned for, though usually I've only asked for a little bit of equality: If he gets this, then (sometimes) I (might) get that. I never wanted the best of *anything*. Never hoped for it. (Perhaps that was my big mistake.) But I've changed now and there's this sudden, clear view of everything. I'm remembering, too, that I knew somebody else once, both smart and rich, who had sagging breasts just like mine and it made a difference in her life. She confided this to me in a whisper, if you're wondering how I know. She was wonderful even so, moving in masterly slow-motion sometimes, and such an elegant head! So poetic, too! What I think is that if her breasts hung down it *can't* be all wrong.

Profiles of middle-aged woman-poets drawn from life:

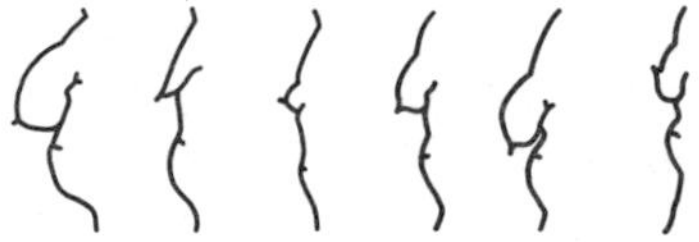

They are all treasures!

My profile:

The possibilities of poets are endless.

Is the back of my head really elegant enough? It might be. *I* can't tell. If it is, then maybe I'm trying too hard to be that kind of strong, silent, charismatic woman-of-the-world-with-secret-sorrows when I really don't have to make such a big effort. I should keep reminding myself that women can be immense! That there are royal women, African queens, white (and black) goddesses. Many of them make lots of little mistakes and never even apologize at all. But I am small. I am, in fact, a *small*, dark, brooking stranger, having ridden a horse only once or twice and Mr. Rochester never notices the back of my head; so if I do relax and stop trying so hard, it's up into the tower for me for at least some part of every day and certainly on weekends whether the children are home or not.

Before continuing, I want K to know that (so far) I've never done anything reprehensible (especially not to the children or in front of them) and not even any crazy thing that caused irreparable damage, and if I did, it was a long time ago. I forgive myself and I forget it. Even my recent outbursts shouldn't stand between me and real life. Would that be fair? And did anyone ever stop to think how hard Mr. Rochester is to live with sometimes?

I am, by now, standing in the doorway of the castle, though only the back door. It's the kind of small, unassuming door that might be for poets and musicians to come in and go out by without fanfare. Probably unlocked. I'm standing beside it, wanting a brand-new (old-fashioned) sweetness like a Beethoven slow movement and a real love story, the kind you can't have anymore, with maybe no sex, but the glimpse of an ankle . . . a very, very beautiful ankle. Mine (both) have little blue veins and permanent black-and-blue marks. Mr. Rochester is also aging fast.

Strange that when Kafka wants to have a picnic, he has it in the shadow of the castle wall right near this little artist's back door instead of out under a tree. If he wants to be polite, correct and, above all, legal, what's he doing here? He must know perfectly well that all the land around here belongs to whoever lives in the castle and might, for all he knows, be mine. I cheer up when I finally catch his eye and since I want to correct any impression he might have that I'm not from the castle, I lean possessively against the door. I know that if I'm not from the castle, he doesn't want to waste his time with me. Or if he does, it won't be "serious." He wants to be in with the "in" crowd and he's tired of feeling cockroachy. Some significant gesture on my part is necessary and right now.

"Well," I say, "I guess I have to go home," and I open the back door of the castle and walk in. I forgot that I may not be from the castle anymore than Kafka is, though in my present state of mind, that seems unlikely. Well, I'm glad I did it even though at that moment—that very moment of the meaningful gesture—I wasn't thinking of myself as the dark, mysterious stranger—but more the other kind, the one everyone is always a little bit contemptuous of, as though I must be the wrong color or too tall for a woman or not properly dressed or somebody too old to bother with or it's that my speech reveals where I come from (which might be Brooklyn).

Kafka, I notice, doesn't follow me in. He doesn't dare. I was afraid of that. He's always so legal and properly dressed!

But let me say that I have always wanted to be left out in the woods by myself, starving, in order to have a vision like the Indians did. I have always wanted to go into the forest almost as empty-handed as I am right now, a little frightened, too: the sounds of rats or squirrels, and strange rustlings that cannot be accounted for. I've always looked forward to some scary place just about like this one, full of bats and swallows and their droppings, so I'm glad I'm here; but also, I've found out something K ought to know and I must tell him soon, though not right now. Something very important to him and interesting to me and that is that there is nobody in the castle. There is *nobody* in the castle! . . . at least as far as I can tell.

Camped on the edge of a vast living room, probably on the site of past slights or little domestic altercations never forgotten, camped between hallway and great hall as though between man and wife or between any who used to be lovers, I have discarded, on principle, everything I might take comfort in: my wedding ring, for instance; my amber pendant given to me by Mr. Rochester; even my watch, by which I could tell the length of the night. There's the tension of verbal battles in the air (I know it so well) and a sense of suffering, sometimes silently, in mismatched marriages. It feels like several generations of them. There's the electricity of the hates of those who yearned for love. I wait, full of unspecified regrets, unspecified desires. It's growing darker. Something flies by. I light two candles.

I have read that in many countries only the men are allowed to have visions.

And now my usual night pains and problems begin: sore neck, tingling hands and feet, skipped heart beats, backache, twitching legs, menopausal sweats. (Perfectly normal at my age.) I think of all the physical things that don't bother me yet but could, and settle myself cross-legged, leaning against the central support of a small table, one of its carved lion paws on each side of me. (They are of no comfort and have no significance to a modern woman like myself.)

Why should I be afraid of ghosts, I wonder? Why, at my age? Or of strange, dark forces of the night or of the cellar? I, who doesn't believe in them, and who (suddenly) does not underestimate myself? Why, when I'm anticipating *at least* an average vision such as the awesome sight of horses and fire or a flock of flying swans in thunderheads or some other, maybe more abstract vision: perhaps a view across the sky of unadulterated joy and brightness, myself in the middle as some kind of victorious woman, both arms raised up and shouting? (I've done that several times before, but not for any of these reasons.)

If something should happen and I should die here, I want to die with a joke. I've always wanted that. I want to make one funny last remark. I hope I'll be able to think of something at the final moment. It should be apropos, too, so it can't be prepared ahead of time. Also it shouldn't be too long. (I hope nobody interrupts me in the middle or misinterprets it. I won't have time to go on or to clarify.)

But *I* could be something up from the cellar myself and proud of it. Old crone from primordial ooze, hatched from blind desire . . . not necessarily from one great yearning, just several little ones, hatched even from wants that might fairly easily have been satisfied with, perhaps, a modicum of free time now and then. But she's all blind force now, with the violence and fury to match Godzilla or King Kong, having bided her time (in the meantime having yelled out windows and waved her arms, having bided my time until it was too late). (How did such small desires, one might ask, lead to all this passion?)

I didn't understand it at the time, but those were moments of sanity when I raged against the bars and screamed out windows . . . moments of sanity when I would have burned the place down if I could, moments of sanity when I couldn't catch my breath.

"... to be Haunted—One need not be a House—."
—Emily Dickinson.

I turn my head away to see more clearly in the dark, wishing for demons, knowing there won't be any; but if I could call up some devil kind of thing to sell my soul to (if I believed in soul or devil), I'd ask to be five or six years younger than I am . . . tell everybody I'm forty-seven instead of fifty-four, for instance, or I'd even take just three years off. I'd settle for two. (I never ask for much, or didn't used to, and anyway, I'm not sure I'd ever like to be thirty-five again.)

I turn my head away to see more clearly in the dark. This is a test.

But perhaps I should ask for more just to raise the stakes, as it were. Aim higher. This is a test and *this* is the test of it right here. I thought the object was to win through in spite of privation, weakness, fear and loneliness — but *what's to win*? (I used to wonder that, even long ago, locked up in the tower. Where were the rewards for good behavior or hard work?) So what's to win now? That's the question and I think answering it is passing the test. So, a couple of thousand dollars would be nice. Or a whole new wardrobe. One perfect moment. (Everybody should have one, though it can be over before you realize it or you may forget you had it right after it happens and then you may think you never had one in your whole life up to now. Also there are always a few flaws . . . expecting sunshine and getting it, but too much wind.) So what's to win now? Nothing that *I* know of. I can feel my vision coming. I hear the thunder of it and I already, now and then, raise my arms up, feel an urgent need to shout. But what if by the time I have my vision I'm too weak from hunger to make it out the door? That's *another* question. Mr. Rochester is locked up and K could never, never bring himself to enter the castle to save me and he's the only one who knows I'm in here. I might die here. I'll have to save myself as I did once before, get out while I still can, as I got out then. Also I've *already* made the big changes in my life, the ones that having visions are supposed to make. Also K will never learn that there's nobody in the castle unless I come out and tell him.

Out then, into the night air — now while I still have the strength to do it — and on, for all I know, to *larger* castles with even *larger* living rooms. I am not harmless. I will not be harmless nor will I be sent back into any towers no matter how tall, my hands tied and without knives or matches. I will fill my own sky. I nearly saw that. I nearly had that a vision. I mean instead of all those swans and horses . . . expecting sunshine . . . a few flaws . . . and I almost had one almost perfect moment . . . .

Verging on the Pertinent

I AM THE WOMAN OF THE YEAR this year, or so it seems so far. It's not easy, though, and I haven't told them I'm older than I look and that I'm "experienced" if you know what I mean, have even had children. Somehow I sense that they would be deeply disappointed not to be able to think of me as virginal, perhaps they would even be enraged and dangerous if they knew I wasn't as pure as they think I am.

I can't speak their language (except what I manage out of my phrase book) and I don't know how any of this happened or why, but from what I *think* I understand, their legends foretold the coming of a handsome stranger just such as I. I come from the suburbs of a large, midwestern city (rather like Detroit) and I appeared, as it were, out of the blue, descending from an Allegheny Airlines plane on a clear day in September—the month for beginnings all around the academic world. This is to be the case with me, it seems—unless instead, this is some sort of an ending.

My hair is orange-red and I believe fire is meaningful to them on many levels. I suppose my saucer-hat may well represent the world as they know it. Of course my right breast the sun and my left breast the moon or something of the sort. My hands, perhaps two white birds of peace, while the large mole on my cheek is certainly testimony to the basic earthiness, the all-too-human quality of my good looks.

I remember that their equivalent of four French horns blew for me that first day and my cigarettes were confiscated in the interest of my health.

The first words I learned in their language were: "Who, me?"

I knew well enough to be humble, flustered, tearful, shy, etc., and to smile with a trembling chin, but for some reason I wasn't really that surprised at being chosen THE one out of so many others. I've always expected something of the sort would happen to me, been waiting for it, in fact; however, I was never quite sure whether it would come about because of my looks or my brains and, actually, I'm not sure which now. For all I know, I may merely be the millionth visitor to arrive here, or as seems more likely considering the place, the ten thousandth, or maybe they just picked an arbitrary number to celebrate. Their ways are so different. How would I know?

So far this year that I've been chosen, the traffic accidents are down by ten percent. Murder, on the other hand, while down in one village, is up in several others. The weather has been dry and unusually hot. Two people were discovered dead of unknown causes. I found the words for "Don't blame me" in the phrase book, but I think they do anyway. Perhaps I'm not pronouncing them properly, and sometimes I think they interpret what I try to say any way they want to. (Rape is up drastically and I can't help wondering if I *do* have something to do with that, considering my body, considering the way I move, and considering my long red hair.)

I would like to learn to say "But I am your leader" or "Take me to him," except the words aren't in my phrase book.

I would also like to make an announcement about myself. I really would. Confess my age and my shoe size. Confess my dyed hair, my long, phoney fingernails; confess my children and maybe say something about the psychology of people who come here, as I did, innocently as tourists: their needs, their expectations, their misunderstandings . . . .

I have been trying to analyze the situation: Am I free to go, for instance, or not? Will I, by any chance, be forced to take part in strange ceremonies where I have to make love to an old goat, non-figuratively speaking? And what happens at the end of the year? Will I have to jump naked into some ice-cold lake with a lot of jewelry on?

I should mention that I have been on several centerfolds of several of their magazines, all with short biographies mentioning my interest in photography and gourmet cooking. None of it true.

And all this time I have been crossing and recrossing my legs, pointing my toes at desirable men, not knowing if that is permissible here or not. Once, as a bold invitation, I even held a teacup in my lap—without the saucer!

My credit cards have all been stamped VOID. I think it may be their way of keeping me from getting out of their country.

They've put me up in their very best hotel. Perhaps I am no longer to be considered of the middle class. At least I certainly hope not.

I have sent and received several letters to and from my husband. He wonders if any of this is really true, if I'm just pretending to be sort of held prisoner here as the woman of the year. He says why don't I just walk out of there, but I'm not sure I can. I told him eunuchs stand at every doorway (they might be eunuchs) and I don't know if they're just symbolic or not. He wrote back that of course he'd rescue me in a minute himself if he thought anything were really wrong or if there were any real danger, but he wants me to learn to solve my own problems, to learn to be more objective and less emotional about my situation and, most of all, to stop exaggerating. He thinks it would be bad for my personal growth if he came to the rescue now. Actually he has always wanted me to be more independent of him, keep out of his way with the little domestic things that come up so often with children and refrigerators and so forth. This, he says, isn't any different from my usual problems and most likely the whole thing's my own fault anyway, or just some kind of misunderstanding. Most of the things I get myself into are and, besides, he's busy.

I suppose he's right, as usual. I may have led them on unconsciously: acting shy, demure, yes, but also wearing low-cut dresses decades too juvenile for me and perhaps, in some ways, just being myself is too much for any normal man to take. (I should mention that my breasts are quite large . . . extraordinarily large in fact.)

Already there have been several rehearsals for strange ceremonies where I am to appear suddenly on balconies or at the top of long, curving stairways wearing see-through gowns, and there has already been one sold-out celebration of myself as heroic womanhood, or at least that's what it seemed like where I inadvertently took a very lascivious pose. I don't blame myself for that. It may have been the music or perhaps the setting or the power of suggestion.

I have heard sudden, single cries of, "WONDERFUL!" in the middle of the night and woke up wondering if I'd dreamed them.

That's what I've always wanted to be. But even Mother never said, "What a wonderful baby girl," at least not that *I* knew of. Once, just once, my husband said, "You're wonderful," but he took it back the next day because of something I did. I forget what. (That was before we were married.) But sometimes I have seemed to myself to be just a little bit wonderful if looked at in a certain particular and perhaps peculiar (dim) light, and once, in a hospital, a kind anesthesiologist held my hand and stroked my face before putting me out. "Count down from *won*derful," I thought I heard him say.

Wonderful is nice, but I'd also like to be in some sort of policy-making situation, though I suppose you can't have both. Anyway, I do keep making proclamations, many of them unquestionably for the betterment of the human condition and I do not mean my own. I have not been selfish about this, but so far I don't seem to be able to make myself clear. I have pieced together phrases in their language out of my little book and I have said everything slowly, loud and emphatically, too, trying to get their attention, sometimes stamping my foot or banging on their equivalent of a table. They made it clear to me that I'm cute when I'm angry, and that's nice and might even be a part of being wonderful, but all my talk seems to be glossolalia to them and I think they like it that way. I wish I could get through to them. Often it's almost as if I were talking to my husband.

Sometimes I wonder, Are they laughing at me behind my back?

Sometimes I try to melt their hearts with my smile.

Sometimes I still, and almost without thinking, point pencils at my crotch.

Sometimes I try to make clear that all women should have their breasts examined every few months, not just the ones built like me.

Now they are flying my best black bra from their flagpole. I like to think it means help, but I know that's too much to hope for and quite unlikely. Perhaps it means danger. What *does* it mean, I wonder?

I seem to be raising basic questions of manhood with my body and my manner and especially with my breasts, though I never asked for ones quite as big as these are and told them so. They've made it clear to me that that's no excuse and that I will have to supply, in some form or other, an answer to all men and before the end of their year, too. It's clearly my responsibility though I don't know why and I don't know what to say or do about it, and especially, I don't want to be misunderstood when I *do* do or say something. I suppose it's a kind of sphinx riddle: "What question is it has for answer, woman?" kind of thing, and especially a woman built like me. Just to be one certainly doesn't make me know the answer though they seem to think it does. I suppose one should be grateful that they even thought of asking, though, of course, they don't really want the answer to women, but rather to themselves as men in some sort of juxtaposition to women, or rather in opposition to them. The question is, Are these breasts and hips, this slender waist, for them or for me? I may never be able to answer their questions. I may just stand here pulling out my gray hairs and relying on tears.

When you have breasts this large I don't suppose you can be choosy about the sort of life you lead. Actually, they do not loom so large in my own world as they seem to in others. I see them at an angle. They don't impinge on my view to any great extent. I could forget about them for days at a time I'm sure, if people would let me. Sometimes I lean them against a table and am completely unaware of them. Sometimes I lean them against somebody's shoulder and don't even know I'm doing it.

In one of their ceremonies I know for a fact that they're going to imitate my walk and wear cut-in-two coconuts on their chests or grapefruit under their shirts and talk a lot of crazy talk that's supposed to be like me. I wonder if that's supposed to be some kind of a lesson . . . if I'm supposed to learn from that? At any rate, I hope their antics mean I have some redeeming social qualities.

I have a fear that at the last minute of that last sacred ritual, the one where they will ask me that last important question about themselves . . . I have a fear that I may forget how wonderful I am and want to be, and that I may cry out in some unfeminine way. But I don't want to shirk all that my body implies even if I don't understand it. I must (mustn't I?) take the consequences of myself as best I can, with courage and serenity. Being wonderful was never easy. I must try hard, though I can't see how I can really be much of an example of the generative principle at my age in spite of other attributes I may have.

But I wonder if, on the other hand, I am to be, in that very last ceremony of all, the mysterious woman, all in black, who leads men to their doom, perhaps wearing a necklace of hands and hearts? Or is that wishful thinking?

"There . . . er she go . . .ooes . . . ." But here I come now, hair piled up in that studied uncombed look, a stray curl or two carefully loose at my forehead. Their clapping sounds like waves. It fades and waxes. Are they laughing ceremonial laughter? Are they winking those ceremonial winks? There's that age-old street-corner whistle! I, as I always did, walk by not looking but doing whatever gets the most applause. Is it the time now for some kind of an answer to myself? (If I do get that answer right, I'd like my reward in credit cards.)

I should have asked my husband a long time ago if he knows anything about this question, though I doubt if he does and he might not want to talk about it anyway.

I'm wondering, Am I going to have the right to be wrong and, if so, how many times? I hate to make mistakes, especially if men are watching, and they always are.

But I may have it all backwards. (If my husband were here he'd say it wasn't the first time.) As far as I know, *I* might be the one that gets to ask for explanations. That's not unreasonable, actually, because the sphinx was a woman. It might be the men that are the ones that have to come up with a quick answer. I should take several deep breaths and try to appear inscrutable (as I suppose I am to them anyway). I will be kind. I'll extend the time limit. I'll even let them make a few mistakes and I may accept any halfway-decent reply they can come up with. (I always have.) But then my moods change fast. I may not.

That is, if I *do* get to be the one out in their desert asking the questions.

If Not Forever, When?

IN THE BEGINNING there was a goddess from whom all things flawed flowed. Pretending to be sure of herself, she made a man. She chose a turk's-head squash for the head, bamboo for arms and legs. She liked the knee joints (apples) and the belly button (a lentil). She used old gold pieces for eyes. It was a sacrifice, but she wanted him to have eyes as golden as a toad's, and she *wanted* to sacrifice. Into the mouth she blew her own hot breath and called "Man, man" — in a loving way, of course, for who would come to any other kind of call — but he didn't wake up.

She thought of names, then, to summon him forth by: Sir Delight or Daylight or Midnight Blue. Mister Old Gold, Mister Pleasure-in-the-Morning, Mister Radish. Nothing worked, but she did not despair. She knew that always the proper word comes first, as "meadowlark" and then the lark. (It is the word that differentiates it from some other, lesser bird.) She was not in a hurry. There were many things yet to consider, as: How instill a scorn for commerce? How instill a passion for art? She knew, as was already written, that when — or if — he did come to, he would "immediately experience, first fear, and then desire." When that desire came, she wanted to be ready to imprint him with herself. She needed for him to follow her everywhere. She wanted him to wake up and find her dancing there, with her green goddess-scarves. Unfortunately the phone rang and, at just that moment, the golden eyes opened. It was the sound that woke him. She was in the next room answering the phone.

The first thing he saw was himself in the mirror she'd brought in to check up on her own dancing. She had wanted to make sure his first sight of her would be at her most graceful. One would think, by this first view of himself, that he would be narcissistic like the rest of us, but he saw his big red head which frightened him. First fear, then, as was predicted. After that, desire; and he was attracted to the glassy surface of the mirror rather than to his image in it, and hence, to all things with sheen and sparkle and depth, including the pupils of eyes, windows, puddles, bubbles, clear soups, chrome, rhinestones, ice cubes . . . . It was a good thing she wore glasses.

The world had already been formed by then, the ground below and firmament above, New York on one coast, L.A. on the other, complete down to the tiniest blade of grass.

His first words were: "I want," and after that, "I go." (Inside she'd sewn up *Webster's Third International* to give him ballast, and he could spell as well as speak.)

Already he'd started for a door, but it was the closet so she had time to lock the front one. "I go?" he asked, realizing his mistake and then he reached to hold her hand but missed. She had pulled back because she wasn't sure who he was yet. She knew his being cannot yet have blossomed and was still but a tiny dot (which is as we all begin). And she knew she hardly knew him (what was there to know so far?), but already she felt pain as if her lover or her youngest son was leaving. "You need guidance," she said, "even the suburbs will destroy you, not to mention the city. And you have no money and no knowledge of it. You might have to trade your eyes for nourishment and then you would lose your hope and your good red color."

He said, "I will not squander this present moment with thoughts of other moments no less nor more important than this very one."

"At least tell me your name before you go." (Perhaps with the name she would have some control.) She was thinking she wanted to kiss his imitation lips because she'd drawn them so fine and so full, but when he turned and looked straight at her, she noticed that she'd set the golden eyes much too close. Even so, his luminosity was not like any other living squash she'd ever seen.

"I am just this which I am, as you see."

Oh, my God! she thought. He has said "I am that I am," or might as well have. I have fashioned my own master. This always happens. (She had already born six chiefs of state.) She knew that were he an ordinary person, he would not be saying, "I am" so soon after coming into being. She wondered if she had fallen in love with him for that reason — for that great "I am" — or if it was mainly because he wanted to leave her.

This time when he reached for the door she let him. In less than five minutes he'd figured out the locks and the doorknob and started down the stairs. She followed as she was, in her green goddess-dress, taking only time to grab her purse and running shoes. On the table in the hall she'd left the squash seeds from when she'd hollowed out his head in order to fill it with the good brown broth of thought. She had roasted them and salted and buttered them. She grabbed those also so as to have a snack for later.

Though stiff and with jerks — also a limp (she must have made one leg quite a bit too short) — he stepped out into the sunshine like a king, arms raised, fingers spread. "Look," he said, "look." His eyes just then caught the sun and she saw a spark in each one. "Look," he said, "here are the leaves of the trees as well as the branches," for there were trees there, lined up along the curb all the way to Second Avenue and it was spring. "And these are the trunks of them. How unusual."

"No," she said, "it isn't. Besides, the force that causes trees to grow is known." She was glad she had made him a head taller than most men. "I forgot to tell you," she said, "that the world is round and floats in an infinite black sky."

"How unusual," he said.

She said, "It isn't. Look at me, am I unusual?"

"I didn't choose another world than this one," he said. "I didn't choose this nor another one unlike it."

But she was thinking it was she who'd not only chosen him, but everything to make him out of — this particular squash and this particular sugar cane between his legs. And she was thinking she'd rather have lost control of the wind and the tides and the local weather (and that sometimes happened) than of him.

When she saw that he *would* leave, her hope had been that he'd head straight for the art museums, but he turned in the opposite direction. She decided, anyway, to tell him all the ways in which art is useful. "It starts conversations," she said. "It stands for other things. It tells all, and more than can be said in words. It attracts important people. It begins again and again. Sometimes just one single sung note can be of unimaginable length and beauty."

Talking about art made her realize she had dressed him all wrong. She'd thought of dignity instead. She'd given him a navy-blue pin-striped suit with vest, a wine-red tie, white shirt, Homburg. And he did look princely, red and tall and already his beard was growing. A soft, green fuzz.

Just then a sparrow flew down and perched on his shoulder. She was thinking that this was unusual, but she didn't want to say it, and anyway, before she could, it flew off. She was pretty sure it was a sign of something.

By now they'd reached the corner. "Watch how everyone crosses when it says MILK," she said, "and how they all don't cross when it says DON'T MILK." She was thinking if she confused him he would need her more. Also, surreptitiously, she began to nibble at the squash seeds, thinking in that way to gain some power over him. "Red for go," she said, and, "There are as many mysteries as there are shades of green."

There, in the sunshine—and he having had a sparrow on his shoulder—she was thinking she was glad she had made him even though she'd always preferred manageable miracles and, if any, only tiny flaws. And she thought that though he limped, he walked and talked as if he were lord of the stuff that holds the birds up. But she wouldn't call him that, even if those were the only words there were to stop him and bring him back. Lord of Air, indeed, and he already too proud and not yet in this world half an hour! Perhaps she should trip him. Have him fall down right there in the gutter. Show him just how much the air held up a thing like him. It would be a favor to him in the long run. And she did that, catching his heel from behind with her toe in a way she knew how to do, so that his own left toe hit his own right heel and he thought he'd tripped himself. He went down but got up just as proud as ever, though limping a little more than before so that she thought maybe it would suit her purposes better if she just told him about his imperfections, from close-set eyes to naiveté. He walked as though he didn't have a single fault. It was ludicrous. Who would ever love him? But of course she did. And what she ached to say was that, and call him "Lord of the See-Through Air," and say "Glory, glory. Holiness is in you." (And, anyway, who else was there to love just then?)

But where was he off to like this? Did he believe in *do* not *be*? (One wouldn't suspect this of vegetable matter.) But better to move around and do, than be some vague hero of the contemplative life, whether artist or not.

There were shop windows now along the Avenue. Often something glittering in them made him pause: stainless steel pans, a dress all sequins, eyeglasses . . . . "Do you want a pair?" Eggs, she called them. "Do you want some of those eggs?" (Perhaps she could win him over with a gift.) He picked tortoise-shell frames and pinkish lenses and seemed so pleased with himself that she tripped him again and the glasses fell off and he stepped on them and they broke. "Look what you did," she said, and said that he should watch where he was milking. Here, in the shadow of a building, without the glint of the sun, his golden eyes were blank. All surface. Vegetal.

"Are you unhappy?" Searching his face in vain for signs of sadness.

But even in this light she was struck by his beauty. Perhaps it was exactly those flaws that made him so attractive, or perhaps because she'd made him *by hand*, one piece at a time (it showed), and she'd not considered the consequences (though when had she ever?). Let there be ambulatory vegetal matter, and there was, and let nothing obviate its vivid originality. Let such things shine forth (in their own natures) as pumpkin, apple, maidenhair fern.

"If you're unhappy, art can give you joy," she said. "Art laughs a lot and is full of non sequiturs. It's a chance to rise above the everyday or, on the other hand, get back down to it. A cow might moo no better than MOMA." She doubted MOMA was in *Webster's Third*. All the better then if he thought she'd said, "Mama."

He took a right and then a left and she thought maybe he was, after all, headed for the Museum of Modern Art, or maybe, though she hoped not, Macy's or Altman's. She almost praised him for, at least, a step in the right direction, but it turned out he was going to the Empire State Building. How steer him away from it?

"Did I already tell you that art is short and for our time? We must hurry. Everything changes." But he didn't hesitate.

It was her breath, damn it, the first breath in his lungs. That would be true even if it turned out he really was — and she still wasn't sure of it — *was* the Lord of Air, and yet now hardly a backward glance at her and not even an answer. "If you must go up, at least take the elevator. There'll be a good view all the way to Long Island, but is that art?" she said, and, "The air's no cleaner up there than down here."

She grabbed his arm, but she'd made him of strong resilient stuff. He jounced her off and started up the stairs pointing with the first fingers of each hand and saying, "Pot, pot." She had no idea what he meant and she knew it was her own fault.

"Don't you even know what an elevator is? You don't even know."

At the seventh landing she was already out of breath but she managed to grab the back of his suit jacket. "Well, what *do* you think about art then?" She was trying to slow him down with talk. "Maybe you think it's not for the masses. You think air is democratic. If you can spell at all you know there's not that much difference: art or air, — air, art. Maybe all there is up there is nothing but polluted art from here to New Jersey. The sky so yellow all the eggs in the world won't help."

But he didn't slow down much even with her hanging onto the back of his coat like that, though she saw the dull gleam of his eye as he looked back. Duller than ever here on the stairs.

"Lord of Art," she said, "Art." That got to him. "Arty?" she said, thinking: airy, airborne, aerie, aeronaut, wings . . . . "You can't fly. I hope you know that. I hope you have that much sense."

What he answered was, "If I understand the universe, it is unusual and it is up."

"It isn't. The universe is no more there than right here." At least he wasn't climbing quite so fast. "Taken even one day at a time, you know, life is incomprehensible. We can't unravel the secrets of a single hour. Choose the happiness at hand. If not love now, then when?"

But he had pulled away from her. Well, there was an easy solution she should have thought of before. She took the elevator from the sixteenth floor and waited for him at the observation deck. By the time he came she'd eaten all the squash seeds. How many years of bad luck would that mean?

He had those same blank eyes. Had she just not noticed that in the beginning because of the sun? "Are you unhappy?"

She could have called him Lord of the Evening Air right then and there, and whether true or not, she knew it would please him. Later she always said she had the power to call him back and had always had it, and had it until the very last minute; but right then she didn't know what was important anymore, air or art, or even which was which or what could set fire to the land or move hearts the most: love or money, money or love, and what little she had of either she couldn't spare. At least not without some discussion.

"I had this dance prepared," she said, "but I never got a chance to dance it. Watch this. Watch my scarves. It's air in all its aspects. It won't take long." And she began to do that dance she'd wanted to be doing when he woke. When she caught the flashes of the sun's rays — the setting sun by now — she thought he was watching and she twirled and pirouetted faster and faster until she was too dizzy to stand up. When she stopped, though everything was turning, she could see that he was already up almost to the base of the spire, hanging on with only one hand and still pointing up, though the gesture was wavering. She had been dancing for nobody but herself.

Everything was spinning, but she had the thought that plant life turns towards the sun and heads right out for the universe as fast as it can. It always does.

"Wait," she said. "You need grounding."

She thought she heard him mumble, then, "Let there be light," as though in some doubt about it. Surprising since, though evening, it was still light. And then he was off. She didn't know if on purpose or by mistake. For a moment it seemed as though he hovered in the air and she thought she saw the sun as hat or halo, just before the wind took his coat tail and the flapping sounds began. She didn't have time to wonder whether fall or flight. There was just that split second in which to make a decision. There was just that flash and — reddish, flecked with gray, black — something flew by. Osprey, condor, or some other endangered species, rising from the navy-blue suit.

She would stay up there now and watch the sunset, and after that stare at the stars (though she knew they were nothing but other suns) wondering who, after all was said and done, brought existence into being and continued to cause things to occur, here, or anywhere else? But she would try again (as she always did). She wondered if she wanted slave or master? Son or lover? Mister Radish or Mister Ion — Mister Neutron? Or Lord of the Poisoned Lakes and Sky?

Queen Kong

LIFE, WHEN SEEN as though through the eyes of small women or when looking at a small woman . . . the close attention to details, for instance, or the taking-pains-with of small women wherein even the monumental can be made, fundamentally, minute . . . the elegance of tiny women as they closely scrutinize, nearsighted, squinting over tiny stitches or tiny brush strokes. . . . This is the essence of art, and moreover, art within which the actual function of being a woman is similar (if not identical) to the function of art. Tiny women, then, and with their hair down — on the one hand, adding themselves to the paintings and sculptures of men, or on the other hand, lending themselves to magicians in order to be raised into the air on platforms with no visible supports. Preoccupied with texture, they exhibit themselves on the passenger seats of cars wearing ornate hats. Preoccupied with gesture, they put on shoes that prevent them from taking any steps not in keeping with an organized whole.

Large women, however, do not have the capacity for art. They are anti-art women. Even their breasts are impossible to think about. They are neither art (no matter where or how they lounge about) nor quite real-life either. They are against all elegances, and no wonder, when even seeing them at a distance or simply in silhouette is unnerving. But the potential of large women! The huge, unrealized potential! Their great longings, their colossal grudges, their long-term memories, their rage! No wonder they deny all art . . . deny all civilization and try to convince their tiny, more discreet sisters to join them.

Men have already (and long ago) gone in search of the smallest woman in the world. She was found in a tribe living far beyond the pygmies. Men marveled at her tiny breasts which were exactly in proportion to her size. They marveled at her tiny vulva, at her tiny ways of thinking, at her small, feminine conclusion exactly in proportion to her tiny breasts (as was expected). Men have not, on the other hand, gone to look for the largest woman in the world. They have not entered that jungle, crossed those mountains, those deserts, those vast lagoons. . . . They have not marveled at her largenesses, at the huge perfection (imperfection?) of her nostrils, at the size of her ears, at her eyes, that *really* seem like pools.

She, however, has arrived here in the largest city hoping nobody will notice, and no one has. Nobody glances up and back or turns around, and that's not so surprising since she's hunching her shoulders, squatting down, one hand on the sidewalk, other hand trying to keep the lower part of her hair from tangling in the upper branches of trees. Seeing her, therefore, one doesn't think: My God, here on this very street, the largest woman in the world! but rather, glances aside, hoping for a better view of what's behind her. (And this, in spite of her rather handsome face.) When she is seen, however, with a sprinkling of light and shadow and partly behind a medium-high wall, eyes carefully avoiding eyes; or when seen after she has come around a corner fast and having slipped to the ground in a fairly deep puddle, she becomes almost accessible to the average man. But even so, if one of these days this average man or even some other above-average and taller man takes a liking to her, sooner or later he will notice that she makes him look small even when he is standing in the foreground. But then, she doesn't expect real love, though perhaps marriage is not out of the question.

There is a magician, quite a small man, really, who looms large on stage in top hat and tails. He had a close call with a tiny woman once and now is willing to make do with a large one. Since he's so small, but looks so huge, the largest woman in the world is hoping he can help her achieve an illusion, not only of refinement and artistry, but most particularly, he should be able to change the gargantuan to the merely large by the use of strategically placed lights and mirrors. (She already knows she should dress on the bias and use at least three colors.) She'd like to be coaxed and taught and goaded by this little man and yet give satisfaction . . . long-term satisfaction, but being neither small nor artistic, how do that? And what *do* men want, anyway? (Freud's perennial question) What do men *really* want, and are they never satisfied, going as they do, from woman to woman?

What are they searching for? And why is it that just when things have settled down nicely, suddenly some other woman is required, or two or three, each one smaller, younger, and more artistic than the last. But their ultimate goal is never reached. That smallest, youngest, most artistic—and therefore most desirable of all—is somehow not found. (Perhaps we must leave the answer to Freud's question to the poets.) How, then, can she ever hope to give long-term satisfaction, having, of these three attributes, only youth, and youth for so short a time? But can she encourage a man's feverish attempts at meaning and grandeur? Can she follow directions? Give constant approval? Make minimal demands? And at the very least, *keep smiling*? But the questions are by now merely rhetorical since the largest woman in the world has already married the magician. She married him quickly before he found out her shoe size.

That feeling when you're just a little bit drunk and you can suddenly HEAR . . . you can hear the ambience of a place . . . every little sound having meaning and a strange clarity. That's the way small women hear things *all* the time. Notice every tinkle and thunk and respond to the inner implications. But she's much too large for that kind of listening. Eardrum's thick tickle. No finesse. Can make out only the lowest notes of any given piece of music. Eyes can hardly trace the line of demarcation between a leg and a hat in any given work of art. Where's the artistic fulfillment in that? And what about the leisurely enjoyment of tiny cupcakes served on fine china? What about whispered catch-phrases . . . the flash of a signal that might be meant for her? And now, already a whole year has gone by and no art done. Nothing to show for it, not even one little clay pot or a part of a quilt or a sweater, not even a scarf to give to her husband. And everything refined or polished keeps slipping out of her hands, falling to the floor, and she steps on it. It's more or less the same with all the impedimenta of everyday life. The knobs and switches made for finer fingers: her husband's little dirty socks, his little bits of food and drink, his slippery little penis. (She sat on his glasses. She stepped on the cat.) How can she be expected to keep track of the details of life even though, as a wife, that's her main job?

What she'd rather be doing is taking some part in his magic show. Go on stage with him. Stand beside him in the spotlight (all in sequins). Be sawed in half. Curl up in a box and have swords stuck into it. But she shouldn't have to ask. He should ask her. He should have asked her a long time ago.

But now it is interesting that she longs to take a risk of some kind. Risk a grand gesture, perhaps even on stage. Risk . . . actually risk standing up to full height, aiming for the monumental mode. (It is clear that she suspects that she might be numbered among the ten tallest women. She wouldn't dare think more than that.) And now she allows herself to imagine what it would be like to go on stage with her husband as the featured part of the act, in pink and silver and swinging her tassels. "Ever see . . ." for instance, "Ladies and Gentlemen, ever see a five or seven thousand pound . . . Ladies and Gentlemen, twelve or fifteen thousand pound woman perfect in . . . almost perfect in every detail, though can't be exactly perfect because of the Square-Cube Law, which is why elephants are built as they are and, therefore, why she is as she is? When she steps on stage it is a moment suffused with an out-of-the-ordinary femininity . . . an out-of-the-ordinary roundness and fullness. Some of you may object, saying that while she certainly is female, she is definitely not art, but what is 'not-art'? Good and bad art, yes, Ladies and Gentlemen, but what can be 'not-art' when already pointed out as such? Large as she is, I can assure you she is, nonetheless, much in the company of poets, and that her grief is as boundless and inconsolable as any. Also she's capable of misconceptions as large as any known so far. Capable of sweeping overstatements, of great bewildering and labyrinth conclusions, gross misunderstandings. . . . All, in short, commensurate with her size. Come, Ladies and Gentlemen, and listen to her speak out on the larger issues of the day wearing nothing but a bra and G string, and for just one small extra dollar, topless."

(She is willing to risk all in her daydreams.)

(Actually, if she wants to go on stage with him, she really has no need to ask permission.)

(She could liberate the men's toilets just by looking in the door.)

He had fondled her earlobe instead of her breast. He has sucked at a wart on her neck. He has slid down her body little by little by little, kissing all the way. She had wondered where he was by now. Felt the tickle of him here and there. (It is clear that she is leaving it all up to him . . . letting him make all the discoveries . . . all the wild surmises. . . .) It's fun for her, too, but doesn't fill the days. No wonder she's—and quite suddenly—no longer under his control. Imagine, then, looking towards the window one moonlit night and seeing her huge hand reaching in and picking up a fairly important and rather fat executive who has been working late, and she's half way up the World Trade Center already.

Up on the roof now, and looking down at her, there are several psychologists, all Ph.D.s and all well over six feel tall. They are experts in cases not unlike this one, in which, for instance, some rather large, sad woman will suddenly appear at the top of a flagpole.

"Lack of long-range planning." "Explosion of some inner, narcissistic frustration." "A tenuous hold on femininity." "But what do women want, and in what order?"

It is decided that she should get no special consideration in spite of, or because of, her size.

The man in her fist is the father of three girls. He understands this sort of thing.

Appeal to her conscience (if such exists), asking: "Can a worthy cause be aided by a heap of debris? By fragments of torn flesh and broken bones?"

("Come on down now, Margie, before you hurt yourself.")

Imagine a model of the World Trade Center just a few inches high with a model of this girl halfway up one of the buildings, long hair blowing, torn nightgown, one breast partly exposed. It's not a work of art, but you'd buy it anyway, thinking that what the creature probably needs most is a good lay. Men who are magnanimous by nature think this, and sometimes several times a day, and with spectacular generosity, proffer themselves in a semiprofessional capacity for the act in question. They will say that they do not normally scatter their love in this fashion, though they are obviously not finicky. Perhaps such men haven't yet realized the scale of the operation. Perhaps they see her, in a way, as part of the landscape, therefore to be climbed, cut down, or bulldozed into a shape more suited to their needs. It's an easy mistake to make.

Always, after rage and tears, comes sadness and regrets. Things lapse into their opposites: hate to love, love to hate. And in the same sense, the large always have their smallnesses; the fat their thin; the meek their ferocities; the foolish, their profundity, and vice versa. Therefore she must be feeling awfully small and insignificant by now, being so large. She must feel pretty foolish up there. Who wouldn't? even though we are all somewhat in her situation — if only figuratively speaking (stuck, that is)—and with every direction impossible. Climbing a tower, an act of desperation, a cry for help. What's there to come down *for*, in other words? And if she should go up, why up?

Certainly, at this moment, she is at her most human.

But now, slowly, everything is becoming suffused with a pale, pink light and she has turned a calm face towards the sunrise. A sort of euphoria possesses the onlookers. They are all, yes, as if in love, even though the whole affair is not only in dubious taste, but against the law. Even so, everyone—including the psychologists on the roof—has stopped talking.

Over a loudspeaker the crowd below is being informed that in spite of the transient beauty due completely to the rising of the sun, nothing of any great consequence is or has been happening. Also, that everything is well under control and that that woman will not be allowed, under any circumstances, to remove her nightgown, so there's no danger of that kind of disrespect. (This last is a message to those who had been worrying about it.)

The psychologists say that one must try to invent a future for her however false it may really be, otherwise why would she move at all except to strike out? . . . except perhaps to toss away the fat executive? She must not find out now, in other words, that her husband is filing for divorce, having finally discovered the true dimensions of his wife. Must not let her know that she serves no useful purpose even as the largest anything. Not let her know that a committee for the monumental wants to go her one better. They have suggested that a French woman, depicted as large or even larger than the largest woman in the world and in an even longer nightgown, be put up in the harbor holding a symbolic lamp of some sort and with uplifting words on her plinth, such as "Give me your tired. . . ." Such an idea is patently absurd and we already have too many tired people as it is.

Things take a turn for the worse because now she *has* taken off her nightgown. Torn it away in one big sweep of the hand. Perhaps by mistake. So the giant thighs for all to see, and besides the one big boob, now another, slightly more pendulous, flopping in unison with the first. Don't look. Pretend she's not there. She won't get any sympathy this way. If she wanted to be taken seriously she should have stayed as well-dressed as possible. That's always the best policy, particularly where large women are concerned.

She needs a firm hand, but even so, it has been decided instead to ignore her. It's so much cheaper than calling out the National Guard. Were she the largest man in the world or some huge beast, of course things would be different, but a woman is so easily made to feel insignificant . . . invisible even. The psychologists think one has only to turn one's back for her to withdraw quickly in shame. The spectators are advised, therefore, to read their morning newspapers, but under no circumstances to let her see that she is pictured on the front page. And so all eyes — or almost all eyes — have turned away and many of the spectators have already left to go back to the serious business of the world, some into the very same building she clings to. It is hoped that she will tire of the whole affair and disappear tonight at the latest; though if no one is watching, who will know about it?

But now she *is* moving. At last. Up, it seems. No, not up. Wait. It looks as though she is simply changing her position in order to get a better view of the crowd below her. It's good hardly anyone is watching. Most are obediently reading their papers, though a few stare off into the side streets. She looks puzzled and almost as though she just woke up. And now she stares at the horizon, East, then West.

The solution to ignore her was obviously the correct one. Here she comes, carefully, down. With a kind of elephantine grace she places her big, flat feet onto the road below (one giant step for a giant woman . . . backing down). Perhaps the magician, if he's watching her right now, is having second thoughts about filing for divorce because look at the tender way she places the fat, important executive on the sidewalk and he's only slightly rumpled. See how carefully she steps around the crowd. No harm done. And the building is in fine shape. She seems changed, though. Perhaps it's because she's standing up straight for the first time. Quite a sight, too. The crowd is sneaking looks in spite of the directives not to. They can't help it. Thank goodness she isn't paying any attention to them. She steps out briskly. North. And soon disappears from view. The spectators sigh and fold their newspapers. They know they will have to wait for the six o'clock news to get the rest of the story. Within the hour they will all be back at work. Later they will see pictures of her taken by helicopters as she crosses the George Washington Bridge and heads West on Route 80, walking stolidly. Not looking back. Probably heading for wide-open spaces.

Now some of them are saying that in spite of her size, or because of it even, she has had artistic validity after all. Like writing the longest poem in the world (as has already been done), this might be or, rather, have been — an act on a par with the Spiral Getty laid out in the Great Salt Lake. Well, let her have that small victory and let us get back to the business of the world . . . to our everyday tasks as guardians of the culture as a whole, back to that particular kind of enjoyment that is the enjoyment of small women (and of the smallest woman in the world) whom we treasure. Everyone does admit, though, that this huge woman was not without fascination of a sort. But time does fly. Wherever she is, by now one can assume she is no longer quite so young and so, not quite so interesting. Let her clump around out of sight, then, in a land she is more suited to: Grand Canyon or some giant redwood forest. It's for the best.